KT-460-060

ANIMALS UNDER THE STONE

ANIMALS UNDER THE STONE

Stephanie Baron

Arlington Books
Clifford Street Mayfair
London

ANIMALS UNDER THE STONE
*first published 1981 by
Arlington Books (Publishers) Ltd
3 Clifford Street Mayfair
London W1*

*Typeset by Inforum Ltd Portsmouth
Printed and bound in England by
The Pitman Press
Bath*

*British Library Cataloguing in Publication Data
Baron, Stephanie
Animals under the stone.
I. Title
823'.9'1F PR6062.0516A/*

ISBN 0 85140 524 X

Contents

A Note to the Reader

I was brought up in just such a village as that in which this little story is set. Many of the events described actually took place there, during my girlhood, and many of the characters – though I have given them new names – are portraits, faithful as I have skill to make them, of real people known to my family and myself.

Whatever other merits my little book may be adjudged to have, it can boast at least that of being *true to life* . . .

To a life, alas, long gone. The pages that follow are, perhaps, no more than a small memorial to a better time.

Stephanie Baron

CHAPTER THE FIRST

In Which A Soldier Pays The Price Of Gallantry

It was evening, and beginning to get cold. Leaves fluttered down from the plane-trees which divided the playground from the churchyard; they flopped about the grass in an intermittent breeze, and swirled round the bonfire which the Wolf Cubs were building under the supervision of Major Martin.

The Vicar strode along the edge of the playground towards his church. It was his custom to stride. He might have once been able to walk, or even stroll: but the Godly stride, acquired at Theological College, had become a habit with him. It did not suit a man with legs so short or upper lip so long.

The Vicar was on his way to Evensong. Not many people came to Evensong nowadays, owing to the pub and 2L.O. on the wireless. The hymns, psalms and canticles would sound a little ridiculous: a thin, embarrassed piping hardly to be heard over the organ, a far cry from the joyful shout of the old days, the merry music enjoined on the faithful, the muscular bellowing of the Vicar's own youth at school and college. But the organ would make a noise like thunder, owing to the enthusiasm of Mrs Cathcart.

It was not easy to be a man of God in the godless post-war world. But the Vicar shouldered his cross and strode with an air of steadfast faith from the Vicarage to his church.

The Vicarage was dark. Smoke came from the chimney, but there were no lights to the windows.

"Hold on a jiffy," said the Vicar's daughter, dainty Millicent Willis, who was looking out of her bedroom window. "The other day Father turned round and came back."

"Why? Why did he? He won't come back now, will he? He must be in the church by now, isn't he?"

"Your hands are cold. Brr! They give poor Millie goose-pimples. Do go and warm them in front of the fire."

"Where is the fire?"

"In Father's den, of course. Where do you think we light the fire? In the drawing-room?"

"Right-ho, then, I'll toddle down."

Captain Cathcart, before he left the gay and girlish room, touched Millicent's hair with a tentative finger. It was a romantic gesture, suited to the evening, but not suited to her hair, which was bobbed. Millicent had once been up in an aeroplane, and was in many ways a modern young lady.

She took off her wooden bangles, and watched the Vicar's black hat disappear into the churchyard. The bells stopped. She took off all her clothes, looking out of the window from time to time. It became obvious that the Vicar was not going to turn round and come back. He had not forgotten handkerchief, spectacles, watch or throat-lozenges. Reassured, she went downstairs. It was almost dark on the staircase and in the hall, but the windows of the Vicar's den were full of cold, golden light from the west, and the coal fire glowed in its basket.

"What a time you've been," said Captain Cathcart.

"Well, you haven't got on very quickly," riposted Millicent with an adorable pout. "I sometimes think you don't really care for Millie! I can only give you a quarter of an hour, you know. Doctor Corbishley and Major Martin are waiting in the drawing-room. What do you feel like this evening? Just the ordinary, or something special?"

"Just the ordinary today, thank you, Millicent."

"Right-ho. But do get on with it, old thing."

"Here?"

"Yes. The fire's nice, don't you think? I always like an open fire."

"By George, so do I. It makes a room ever so much more cosy."

Captain Cathcart undressed quickly, starting with his sock-suspenders. He folded his clothes with military precision, laying them in a pile on the Vicar's desk.

Millicent watched him with some impatience, while lying on her side on the hearthrug, toasting her *derrière*. Her delicious buttocks became pink in the heat of the fire. She was a bonny girl, a healthy, old-fashioned country girl. Her breasts were heavy, her thighs copious: she did not altogether fit the 'boyish' ideas of the times. Her coppery hair crinkled rather than curled; worn long, it would have suited a Tintoretto 'Bacchante', or a creature of Rubens, or of Fragonard: a pre-Raphaelite 'Inspiration', or a 'Gibson Girl'. But of course it was bobbed, for even in this remote country village ran the writ of stern Mistress Fashion! Millicent's eyes were wide and periwinkle blue – her mouth small as a mouth should be, but graced with a 'bee-stung' lip – her nose high-bridged yet pertly tip-tilted. Oh, but she was, it may be believed, belle without question of the village!

Captain Cathcart removed his socks last, as though embarrassed by denuding his feet. It was a pity that he had to remove any of his clothes (though the circumstances of the moment required it) because he looked much better in his clothes than out of them. On his appearance, when dressed, he had worked hard to perpetuate soldierliness, the spirit of the one great and happy period of his life; on the whole he had succeeded. Tweeds suited him. He was not really a soldier at all, but in his tweeds, and with his small moustache, he passed for one. But without his clothes he looked like a librarian or pharmacist. His legs were spindly. Hair grew on his body in untidy, haphazard clumps; he looked like a lawn mown by an idiot.

He laid his socks neatly side by side on top of the pile of clothes on the Vicar's desk. He joined Millicent on the hearth-rug.

"I am a naughty boy," he said. "Oh, what a naughty boy I am."

"Do hurry up. The others will be freezing in the drawing-room."

* * *

Doctor Corbishley and Major Martin waited in the drawing-room, looking at everything except each other.

Doctor Corbishley, dressed sportingly in knickerbockers, stood with his hands clasped behind his back, frowning, in the gathering darkness, at a painting of a cow. He was of the Vicar's small stature, of Captain Cathcart's stringy build. He had been a medical student throughout the war, and felt keenly that Major Martin –

perhaps Captain Cathcart also – despised him as little better than a 'conchie'.

Major Martin was in the greatest contrast. He was burly of build, gingery of moustache, bluff of manner. He looked every inch a soldier, though not, perhaps, an officer. He stared at the mullioned windows – almost dark, as the Vicarage drawing-room faced north and east – and thought what a fine old place it was. He was lucky, he knew, to have the 'entrée' in such a house.

After what seemed an age, a silvery voice called for Doctor Corbishley.

The Doctor cleared his throat, straightened his tie, and left the drawing-room quickly, without a backward glance.

* * *

The Vicar took four shillings and eightpence. Millicent took six pounds. She only just got rid of Major Martin before the Vicar got home. Major Martin legged it out of the back door and through the garden. He hurried to The Black Swan to establish his alibi.

* * *

Doctor Corbishley bicycled home to the cottage he shared with his sister. Parts of him got very hot as he pedalled against the wind, but parts also very cold. He wore the mittens his sister Edwina had knitted him, but they did nothing for the tips of his fingers or for his ears. He felt the cold at the best of times. It was one of the ways in which he was at a permanent disadvantage.

His accent was another. His senior partner, Doctor Bland, was one of the old school, and made no secret of his surprise at the way Doctor Corbishley pronounced certain words. By an unfortunate but repeated chance, these words occurred far more often in Doctor Corbishley's conversation than such other words as he pronounced much as Doctor Bland himself did. It was not a very strong accent, as Doctor Corbishley had been brought up in Croydon, not in Stepney or Huddersfield, but it was certainly quite different from Doctor Bland's.

The Corbishleys, brother and sister, had not been asked to dine by Doctor Bland, nor by Captain and Mrs Cathcart, nor by the Vicar, who together might have been described as the aristocracy of the village. (It was now, to Doctor Bland's simulated regret, a village without a Squire.) Edwina felt keenly this social neglect, but Doctor Corbishley did not mind so very much. He was 'a bit of a radical', as he sometimes put it. Besides, he was sure that in those grand houses he would have committed a 'gaffe', or made a 'floater'.

A more serious disadvantage suffered by the worthy young Doctor was his inexperience. Though thirty years of age, he was made to feel hopelessly callow by such a 'blood' as Major Martin, and even by Captain Cathcart, though the latter had a comparatively diffident personality. They had been in the war, which gave them an unfair advantage, especially with women. Millicent had done wonders for Doctor Corbishley's self-confidence (even Edwina noticed a difference) but he could only afford Millicent once a month.

He had tried growing a moustache, to be more like Major Martin and Captain Cathcart: but after a fortnight, although he could feel it, no one could see it. He looked no less like an underfed white guinea-pig.

He put his bicycle in the shed, and wiped his feet carefully on the doormat.

Edwina asked, "Did you have a nice cycle ride, then?"

* * *

"Three 'iss evenin'," cackled old Mrs Monger, peering through her dirty net curtains.

Her window gave on to the Vicarage garden. She did not peep out of it all the time, owing to almost incessant 'calls of nature', but she peeped out of it as much as she could.

"Ar," said Albert, her son, who had not done a day's honest work since his seventeenth birthday five years before.

" 'Er be makin' a mort o' money," said the aged dame, ruminatively.

"Ar."

"Orta be made tew share un wi' them liss fort'nate."

"Ar?" Albert's face showed, if not intelligence, at least the glimmerings of an understanding of what his parent was getting at.

"Fi' pun Oi wants from 'er," enunciated the matriarch. "Yew arst 'er. Gi' yer Mam a fag, yew lazy bastard, afore Oi locks yew up in a dark cupboard."

* * *

"Message for you, Major Martin, sir," said Tom Melhuish, landlord of The Black Swan.

"My better half, I daresay. Ring through, did she?"

There were nine telephones and five motor-cars in the village: for Country as well as Town was blessed by good Dame progress!

Dolly's message was that she wanted the Major to bring back a bottle of British port. It was a ruse. The Major's military training enabled him to see through it at once. She was checking up on his movements, suspicious bitch that she was. There might be a spot of awkwardness when he got home, but bluff would win through.

The Major had been described as an ill-bred bounder. The comment had not been widely made by brother-officers in his regiment, where, in wartime, such things were not much remarked on. But it was more often heard in the renewed scrutiny which followed the Armistice, when things 'returned to normal'. Doctor Bland said it was amazing that the fellow had even been given a commission, let alone promoted to 'field rank'. Doctor Bland said that it showed the country was well rid of Kitchener.

The Doctor's remarks were widely quoted, as the Major had made himself conspicuous by energetic local activity. He ran things like the Boy Scouts. He said, "If you're going to be a country gent, you might as well do it properly." He believed in going the whole hog; he often said so. He made himself much disliked in the village by mucking people about. The Vicar tried to muck people about, too, in a quieter way, with the result that the Vicar was almost equally disliked. The boys did not want to join the Scouts. They wanted to work in garages, wear narrow shoes, and steal things out of the shops.

Tom Melhuish, landlord of The Black Swan, was almost unique in liking Major Martin. He recognised another 'red-blooded man'. They exchanged dirty stories learned far behind the trenches. Sometimes they sang *Mademoiselle of Arment-Years*. Tom Melhuish had been a Sergeant in the Heavy Artillery, and they had many a chin-wag about the grand old days.

* * *

The Vicar was charmed to find that Millicent had made up the fire in his den. She was sometimes thoughtful but sometimes not. The den needed a fire. The Vicarage was a very cold house.

It was not, fortunately, the mansion in which his eighteenth-century predecessors in the parish had lived, the tithe-rich younger sons of the Squire and his friends. That grand edifice had been burned down during the war, in 1916, an act blamed on, but never quite proved against, a woman called Perkup, who claimed that the incumbent of the time had seduced her. The Church Commissioners had decided against restoration of the enormous shell, and against building a large new Vicarage. They had purchased instead a Victorian villa of moderate size, handy for the church, somewhat ecclesiastical in style. It was a seemly dwelling, if damp, and enriched with a wealth of stained glass, in lozenge shapes, in doors and windows.

The Vicar and his 'baby daughter' lived there contentedly, with only a single full-time servant indoors.

"It is more than a house," the Vicar would sometimes say. "It is a *home*."

"It is more than that, Father," Millicent would stoutly rejoin. "It is a *Christian* home."

* * *

"A disappointing congregation," said Mrs Cathcart. "But dear Mr Willis strove manfully."

"Oh. Ah. Aha," said Captain Cathcart. "I'm sorry I didn't feel up to it."

"Two pounds are missing from my purse."

"I say. Two pounds, eh? That's a bit thick."

"I left the purse on the little table in the hall."

"Table, eh?"

"I refer to a piece of furniture, with a flat top and four legs. It is often known as a table."

"Ha ha ha ha ha," cried Captain Cathcart uneasily. "Flat top! Four legs! You'll be the death of me, Felicity."

"That, of course, is what I should like, did not my religious principles put such a thing out of the question. But I should not be doing my duty if I did not punish you."

"Eh? Come now! The servants –"

"Trousers down. Bend over."

"I have not touched your money, Felicity. I would not stoop to such a thing. You are forgetting that I am an officer and a gentleman."

"And your bloomers."

"They are not called bloomers, dear. That word is confined, I fancy, to female undergarments."

"And lift the shirt-tail. Now hold perfectly still."

Husband and wife were in the important drawing-room of Kedleston, the biggest house in the village after Doctor Bland's. Built by a London gentleman in 1905, purchased by Mrs Cathcart in 1919, it combined elegance with comfort, and both with a certain 'air'. Doctor Bland said that it was the only house in the neighbourhood, apart from his own, where he allowed himself to feel *pre-war*.

Mrs Cathcart remembered this precious encomium as she went out into the hall to get a walking-stick. (It was, said Doctor Bland, the only *gentleman's* hall in the neighbourhood, apart from his own, although he allowed that the Vicarage had quite a decent little hall.)

Mrs Cathcart groped among the sticks in the elephant's foot by the front door. Her powerful fingers settled on the sturdy handle of a heavy ash-plant. She withdrew it and hefted it. Satisfied, she strode back into the drawing-room, closing the door behind her.

One oil-lamp glowed with warm and adequate light. Agnes would presently bring another, when she had trimmed the smoking wick. And one day they would have 'electrics'.

Mrs Cathcart stood by the sofa, over one arm of which the Captain had obediently draped himself. She stood, legs apart, Amazonian, measuring the target with her eye. Her backswing was slow. She used the full length of her arm. Hissing with effort, she brought the ash-plant down on the Captain's narrow rump.

He gave a little scream. The note of pleasure enraged his wife. She smote again.

The house-parlourmaid came in, carrying the second oil-lamp. She was well trained by Mrs Cathcart, and knock-ed only on bedroom doors, never those of the downstairs rooms. She put the lamp down in its proper place, on a bead-fringed cloth on the piano. She withdrew, her lip pursed.

Nettled at the interruption, Mrs Cathcart swung the stick at her husband's head. She was a big, strong woman, and her action was excellent. Hockey and lacrosse ('lacks' as they had called it at school) had taught her to put her whole weight behind the swing. The stick hit the Captain on the base of the skull and killed him outright.

* * *

"I never saw such an arse," said the house-parlourmaid to the cook. "Nothing of it. I like a man I can get what I call a grip of."

"So do I, dear, but I never worry about grippin' what's *behind* a gentleman."

"You know what your trouble is? You're coarse, that's what your trouble is."

"What a gentleman has in *front*, that's what I worry about."

"It's a judgement on me, obliged to associate with a person like some I could name."

"A judgement on you? You done wrong, then? You sinned, 'ave you?"

"I been pursued," said the house-parlourmaid loftily. "They tried their blandishments. Where I really likes to get a grip, to tell you the gospel, is by them dangles. They fits the hand like a bell-pull."

CHAPTER THE SECOND

In Which A Butcher Puts The Sabbath To Good Use

Major Martin thundered back to Columbine Cottage in the 'old bus', his beloved two-seater. He had remembered the port.

"I remembered the port, little woman," he said in his manly way.

Mrs Martin – Dolly, to her intimates – looked sulky but formidable. Life had not turned out as she expected. She herself had not turned out as she expected. Daughter of a wholesale grocer in Southampton, she might have made a brilliant marriage. From 1908 onwards she was often on 'the verge', it seemed, of doing so. She had admirers enough, did merry-eyed Dolly – but somehow the ring never did slide onto that plump, pink finger. When the war came she was getting on a bit. It even seemed, to Dads and Mumsy, that she had 'missed her chance'.

But, oh, then, in 1917, the infantry Captain! The bushy moustache, the twirled 'swagger-stick', the tales of the trenches, the hat at a rakish angle, the ardent caresses!

And Dads was so pleased and flattered, and Mumsy was so twittering and brave, and quite a decent allowance was settled on them.

And that was all they had – Dolly's allowance!

Her husband threw away his Gratuity on some get-rich-quick, fly-by-night scheme in the City. And after that, and after being a Major, no ordinary job was grand enough for His Highness – oh no!

So they scrimped and economised, though not very much, as Dads was that generous still. They lived quietly in the country. Quietly! It was quiet all right. They never went inside the houses of the 'toffs'.

All Dolly wanted was to be treated like a lady, and sometimes given a cuddle. But nobody treated her like a lady, and the only one who cuddled her was Ernest Martin – and she *paid* for that.

No wonder she got 'waxy' sometimes.

She said, "Where did you go, before you went to The Black Swan?"

"I took a stroll," riposted the Major, who had foreseen the question and prepared this adroit answer. "Any harm in that? Can't a fellow take a stroll without you jumping down his throat? Nothing healthier than stretching the old legs in the fresh air."

Major Martin beat his chest with his fists, like a man imitating a gorilla, in order to signify a feeling of radiant health.

"I often think," he went on, ostentatiously removing a wrapping of newspaper from the bottle of McGibbons's British Ruby, "that you should walk more, old thing. Put an end to those headaches, in my humble opinion."

"You're the only headache I've got," said Dolly sourly. She pouted, though overweight for such a thing. "Walk indeed. You no more went for a walk. Have you got a girl in the village? That Maud at the greengrocer's? That slut they call a parlourmaid at the Cathcarts'? No more a proper parlourmaid. More like a general slavey. How much did you spend at the pub?"

"Eight and six," said the Major quickly. "Or thereabouts. Give or take a few coppers. I got you that port, you know. I trust you have not forgotten that."

"Then you've still got the two pounds that belongs to the Scouts."

"Certainly! Of course I've got it! I put it somewhere safe. You can't be too careful these days."

"Where is it? I want to see it."

"Certainly! See it you shall. Now let me think. Where exactly did I put it?"

* * *

Mrs Cathcart pondered for a moment. She was too much of a man to panic. She had to make a plan sensibly, and carry it out decisively.

Captain Cathcart hung over the arm of the sofa. His face was buried in the cushions of the seat. One arm hung limply to the floor. The natty tweed coat had ridden up about his shoulders. His trousers and drawers were round his ankles. His backside rose, ivory and hairless in the kindly light of the oil-lamps, the apex of an inverted 'v'. Weals, livid red against the white, marked the impact of the chastising ashplant.

There was a suggestion, in the Major's position, that he was in the process of committing a bestial act, of attempting to ravish the arm of the sofa.

The cook came in suddenly. She had also been trained not to knock on the doors of the downstairs rooms. Mrs

Cathcart realised immediately that Agnes the house-parlourmaid had reported the chastisement 'below stairs'. The cook would have thought up an excuse to come in, but really she had just come to have a look. It was understandable, thought Mrs Cathcart tolerantly, if pert.

Mrs Cathcart's mind worked quickly. She was not one to be dismayed, not one to be found at a loss, not she! She realised that she must conceal, even from her own servants, the fact that she had murdered her husband. She must cause the cook to believe that the wretched creature was still alive.

Accordingly, by way of deception, Mrs Cathcart raised her stick and brought it down, with a hearty smack, on the Captain's buttocks.

"What is it, Cook?" she said.

" 'Scuse me, Mum, but were you wantin' custard or cream with the prunes?"

"Custard. You know the Captain prefers it. I prefer cream, but, as you know, I never allow personal preference to influence my decisions."

"Very good, Mum."

"That will be all, Cook. I do not wish to be disturbed again, until you are ready to announce supper."

"Yes, Mum."

The cook went out. Mrs Cathcart congratulated herself that she had, with word and deed, given the impression that the Captain was still alive.

The next thing was to dispose of the body.

Mrs Cathcart went to the box-room. She knew exactly which suit-case she was looking for, and with the aid of a candle, and with much heaving of other pieces of luggage, she found it. She took it down to the drawing-room, put it on the floor by the fireplace, and tried to fit her husband into it. She manhandled him easily enough – he was a scrawny creature, and she was a games-player, the terror of opposing sides since her early teens.

She found that in order to draw his legs (still bare, and copsed with tufts of ugly hair) up to his chest, she had to lay him on his side in the suitcase. The width of his shoulders then prevented the lid of the case from closing. When, however, she laid him on his back (an indelicate position) neither his legs nor his head could be folded into the case.

Intrigued by the problem, she tried him in all possible positions, wrapping his limbs this way and that. A challenge, she knew, always brought out the best in her.

* * *

"She didn't half give 'im a wallop," said the cook. "Anyway, 'e wants custard with 'is prunes."

* * *

Mrs Cathcart admitted defeat. While it remained in one piece, the body would not fit into the suitcase. Of course, she told herself, it would fit into a cabin trunk, but even she, strongest sportswoman in a dozen parishes, could not conveniently carry a cabin trunk. But the body need not remain in one piece. It could be divided. It would fit into two suitcases, quite comfortably, if she sawed it up.

The thought was father to the deed. Mrs Cathcart was not one to shilly-shally once her mind was made up. Not she! She hoisted the Captain over her shoulder, and carried him upstairs to the attic, where he had his carpentry shop. He made book-ends and pen-holders; the house was full of them, stained and varnished; there were far more book-ends in Kedleston than books for them to support, far more pen-holders than pens to hold. Mrs Cathcart promised herself a bonfire.

Meanwhile, here were saws and chisels.

Mrs Cathcart removed the Captain's clothes, reasoning that one of the dear Vicar's missionary friends might be glad of them. Then she sawed off the arms and legs and head. She was prepared for blood, and spread old sheets to catch it.

But there was far more blood than she expected – far more than the sheets could absorb – far more than she had supposed the Captain's scrawny body had contained. It gushed everywhere over the bare, pine floorboards from severed arteries in limbs and stumps and neck. Mrs Cathcart's fine brow was puckered for a moment in a frown. But for no more than the merest moment! Two birds, Mrs Cathcart cheerily told herself, could be killed with one stone! She had been meaning for ever so long to do something about the bare floor of the attic. There was a paint-brush among the Captain's tools. Mrs Cathcart seized it, and went to work with a will! With a vigorous wrist action learned on the hockey field, she painted the floor-boards with the Captain's blood. The effect was pleasing – a distinct improvement – one of many she could now contemplate.

When her 'paint-pot' was exhausted, as she whimsically put it to herself – when not another drop of the ruby pigment could be extracted for the beautifying of her home – she returned the brush to its jar of turpentine, and turned to scrutinise the pieces of the Captain. She was critical as always of her own efforts. No scamper she, no slapdash anatomist! Something about the torso offended her, an untidiness, the feeling of a job half done. The answer came to her. With a pleased smile she snipped off the tummy-banana (no friend of hers) in the interests of neatness.

She went down to the drawing-room, and brought the large suitcase up to the attic. She secured, from the box-room, another and smaller suitcase. (It was, all of it, *gentleman's* luggage.)

She put the trunk of the body, and its head and arms, in the larger suitcase. In the smaller one she placed legs and naughty bits. She found that, in order to fit the legs into the smaller suitcase, she had to saw off the feet. She put the feet in with the trunk, head and arms in the larger suitcase.

Cook called that supper was ready.

Mrs Cathcart washed, changed her dress and stockings, and went down to the dining-room.

"The Captain is a little overtired," she said. "He has gone to bed. I will make him some cocoa presently. Under the circumstances, I will have cream, not custard, with the prunes."

* * *

Edwina Corbishley cooked her brother a nice vegetarian supper. Afterwards she read him a chapter of *Midshipman Easy*.

Doctor Corbishley was grateful but restless. The mushrooms, picked early that morning among dew-wet cowpats, had reminded him of Millicent's nipples. He had eaten them with a curious, heady sense of conquest. Now he could not get them out of his mind. Millicent's were the first breasts he had actually bitten, although his professional background had naturally made him familiar with feminine anatomy. Edwina had no breasts at all, as far as could be judged from the shape of her clothes, which were 'artistic'. Doctor Corbishley did not think Edwina's nipples, if she had any, would resemble Millicent's. They would not be the size of coffee-saucers, or the colour of succulent fried mushrooms.

Doctor Corbishley thought he would go mad, thinking about Millicent's nipples, and reflecting that a month must go by, at least, before he could once again creep through the Vicarage garden with two pounds in his purse.

* * *

"For what we are about to receive, may the Lord make us truly thankful," intoned the Vicar.

"Amen," said Millicent, devoutly.

Supper was cold, because the cook was away for the day. She went away every Sunday to visit her old mother. It meant a journey. The Vicar had searched his conscience about Sabbath-day travelling, and concluded that he had no convictions in the matter at all. He thought it neither right nor wrong. The question filled him with apathy. He was totally indifferent about it.

"I trust you had an enjoyable ramble, my dear, this evening?" murmured the Vicar, glancing uncomfortably at the bobbed head opposite.

"Not half bad," said tomboy Millicent. "Jolly bracing."

"So I should be disposed to imagine."

The Vicar laughed, since he placed in his life, as in his sermons, a high value on the Christian family, on frankness and unity, on shared sorrow and shared joy.

"I'm ever so sorry," piped Millicent, "that I didn't get to Evensong. How was it?"

"Not thronged. Things are not what they were before the war."

"I suppose Mrs Cathcart made the poor old organ sound like an angry elephant."

"Millicent!"

The Vicar was a little shocked, but he laughed again, uneasily, thinking that the child had a sharp wit, and would bear watching. She would soon be grown up. She would be sixteen in a month or so. She already looked more than sixteen, perhaps, owing to being a big bonny girl, and having her hair done in such a 'grown-up' new way. It was in some regards a pity, for Millicent's sake, that the Vicar's wife had left him, disappearing as she had, suddenly, during a Baptism, with a commercial gentleman from Luton.

What a surprise that had been! But, after the first few moments of amazement, what a joy! The Vicar never failed to give thanks for his deliverance, in his prayers, from that 'Babylonish Captivity'. It was a blessed end to continuous scrutiny and suspicion, especially in regard to the Boys' Club.

Of course Millicent ought still to be at school. But the school had taken so firmly the opposite line, just two terms ago, that here she was at home! Pursuing a course of studies 'by correspondence'! So odd, they had been at the school! So pursed, their lips; so averted, their eyes! Nothing was said right out, and their hints, if hints they were, were quite beyond an anxious father's comprehension. They said Millicent had *outgrown* the school. What was he to make of that?

It was possible to argue that the child was better living in a Christian home, than subjected at school to all kinds of 'modern' influences. But she might get bored and lonely. She did not seem interested in young people of her own age, or in tennis, or mah jong, or 'amateur theatricals'. She took little visible, active enjoyment in anything – in anything, at least, since that episode of the aeroplane, last summer, at Weymouth. That had really taken her fancy. She had only been up for a ten-minute spin, but she found it *most* exciting. The young man, the pilot, had been most kind to her. He took other people up for spins, too, but they had to pay. It was quite a lot of money. Millicent had her spin free! Afterwards she had quite a long talk with the man, in whispers. She said she was thanking him as warmly as her father would have wished.

That evening, the Vicar remembered, she had gone for a walk along the sea-shore, by moonlight. She had, ever so girlishly, insisted on going alone, promising, 'honour bright', to do nothing madcap like going in for a swim. She had come back with rather a lot of sand on her clothes, her hair untidy, her eyes dreamy. She said that walking on the empty beach by moonlight had been a beautiful, beautiful experience.

It was all beyond the Vicar, who had not had a really beautiful experience since the Fifth Form at school.

But the Boys' Club always promised one. It was always possible. If prayer had the power the Vicar believed it to have, why then, one day there would surely come, to enrol himself in the Boys' Club, a little lad something like Morrison Minor . . .

* * *

"Good gracious me," said Dolly Martin, interrupting her own monologue after two hours and eleven minutes 'by the clock'. "Whatever is that?"

"Somebody carrying two suitcases," said her 'Lord and Master', grateful for a change of subject.

"I can see it's somebody carrying two suitcases, thank you very much," cried Dolly, with a touch of asperity. "I am not yet totally blind, although you would no doubt much prefer it if I was, except that I wouldn't be able to work my fingers to the bone for you, much thanks I get. That's Mrs Cathcart carrying those suitcases. I could see her for a moment in the light from Mallinson's window. Toffee-nosed cow, I hope she drops the cases on her feet and breaks her toes."

"Come come, old thing, it's Sunday, you know."

"Whenever I pass her in the village, she looks at me like I was dirt."

"I believe she comes of a very old family."

"Where can she be going to, this time of night, with two suitcases? She could get the carrier in the morning, or go in with the milk, or wait for the bus. Not that I care. You won't catch me prying into other folk's concerns. I've enough to worry me with my own."

* * *

Vic Mallinson was as drunk as a tinker. He always got drunk on a Sunday night. Other people got drunk other nights, but Sunday was his night. Every man to his taste, said Vic Mallinson. Live and let live was his motto. Butchers are not as other men are.

He never went to The Black Swan in the village. That

Tom Melhuish gave him the pip. Forever going on about the bloody war. You'd think there was some kind of glory about being in the army, when all it proved was you were too stupid to stay out of uniform. Vic knew a thing or two, and he had the silver to spend. No call-up for him. He had medical certificates from Doctor Bland (cost a bit, they did), *and* he was doing work of national importance. Catch him being caught by a lot of boobies in puttees. Not Vic. He knew a trick worth two of that. Tom Melhuish thought Vic ought to be ashamed of himself. He was forever going on about it. But Vic knew bloody well he had a right to be proud of himself.

So he went to the King's Head in Bogham, the nearest market town – twelve minutes in the pony-trap going, maybe three hours coming back. Beer and gin he drank, first one and then the other. Or sometimes he had a fancy to drink them both at once. His worries disappeared. He had worries, too, like all conscientious tradesmen anxious to retain the goodwill of their customers by providing a personal service. "Nothing but the best – why go elsewhere?" as he advertised in the Parish Magazine.

Mrs Cathcart was entertaining Wednesday. Vic knew all about it from the cook. The Vicar was coming, that Miss Millicent (bless her pretty face and winning ways), Doctor Bland, all what you might call the rank and fashion of the village. And some nobs from Bogham into the bargain. A grand party, like in the old Squire's time. Blankets of veal; that's what they were having – blankets of veal. Whatever mucked up kind of foreign thing that might be. To serve a dozen. All right. But *where was the veal*? All the calves locally had already gone to Bogham market, except one or two the farmers kept for themselves. There was nothing to be bought on the hoof. So the veal had to be ordered. But there was none to be had! Or, to be more exact, Vic had made a bit of an oversight. The matter preyed on his mind, until he drank enough beer and gin to drown it.

He trundled home behind Bluebell, the old roan pony. (She'd stand up for another year, maybe, then she'd be stewing-steak and sausages, very wholesome.) Bluebell knew the way better than a Christian, and she was used to Vic's singing.

They went through Craddock's Wood. They were nearly home.

Bluebell stopped. She always did hereabouts, this being where Vic was accustomed to make himself comfortable.

"Goo' girl," said Vic.

Reminded by Bluebell, he became aware of the pressure of the beer on his bladder. It was a sort of delightful agony.

He sang a song: "Goo' gel Bluebell, Bluebell goo' gel."

He got awkwardly down from the trap. He fell over and lay for a time on the verge. He stood up at last, supporting himself on the wheel of the trap, and turned to face the pitch-black wood. He might have been and gone straight away there on the verge, but he was a modest butcher. He did not want to risk offending any of his customers who might be driving past in their motors. So he plunged into the thick undergrowth of the wood. He fell over again, tripping on something angular. He swore without heat or rage, since he was quite accustomed to falling over, and did not greatly dislike it. He fumbled for his buttons, the need suddenly urgent. He let go with a sigh of exquisite relief. The beer went on for a long time – the gin, too, no doubt. He signed his name with the invisible jet. He wrote 'Mallinson's Family Butchers for Finest Meat'. He underlined his commercial slogan, but before he could do the squiggles at the corners, as rendered in gold on his shop window, the jet diminished to a trickle.

You can't do squiggles with a trickle. Vic Mallinson sobbed once or twice with frustration.

He stepped backwards and fell over again. It was the same angular object which had tripped him before.

"Grr," said Vic, groping.

It was a box, covered over with leaves. It was a trap, a snare, put there to make him fall over. Tom Melhuish had left a box in the middle of the wood, to trip him up. It wasn't quite a box, more of a case. It felt like a good class of case, genuine leather. It was the sort of thing that might come in useful. It might boil up, and mince down, and go into a pasty. Not the brass bits, of course.

Vic carried the case back to Bluebell and the trap.

CHAPTER THE THIRD

In Which Lad And Lass Meet In The Gloaming

Many people said that the quality of village life had deteriorated. Doctor Bland often said so. He blamed Lloyd George.

Certainly Captain Cathcart's cynical disappearance lent weight to this gloomy view. It was not the sort of way people behaved before the war.

"I blame myself," said Mrs Cathcart to the Vicar, "to a small extent. I was a little short with him, I am afraid, on Sunday evening, after I got home from Evensong. Two suitcases have disappeared. They were my suitcases, as it happens, but I do not wish to dwell on that aspect of the matter. I suppose he took some of his clothes. Yes, certainly, he must have taken a sufficiency of clothes."

"With winter coming on . . ." hazarded the Vicar.

"Indeed. We must begin to expect some cold nights. Have you brought your fuchsias in? And then there are the gladioli to consider."

"And he went, without a word, in the middle of the night?"

"It shows a certain *slyness*."

"It is our Christian duty to try to understand, to endeavour to forgive."

"I hope," said Mrs Cathcart," I am not failing in my Christian duty."

"Shall you go to the police?"

"To Constable Flockett? What purpose, Vicar, would that serve? There will be enough talk, I am afraid, as it is."

* * *

"You know what I keep thinkin'?" said Agnes, Mrs Cathcart's house-parlourmaid, to the cook.

"What's that, dear, obsessin' your mind?"

"It's a good job he wasn't the other way up when she bashed him."

"Ah, but p'raps he *was*."

"Coo."

"P'raps she made 'im turn over!"

"Coo. To think we missed seein' that! No wonder 'e skedaddled."

"It's a miracle 'ow 'e could walk, if she did bash 'im on the front."

"That's just what I was reflectin' on. 'Is dingle-dangles must 'a been squashed out like pancakes."

* * *

"Captain Cathcart, I should say Gregory Cathcart, has disappeared," reported Major Martin to his spouse.

"Fiddlesticks," returned that imperious lady.

"I assure you. The Cubs could talk of nothing else."

"It is Mrs Cathcart who has run away. I should say Felicity Cathcart. I saw her, with my own eyes, carrying two suitcases, walking along this very road, last night. I remarked on it at the time. But of course you never listen to a single word I say."

"No no, old thing. It must have been a trick of the light. It's the gallant Captain who's done a bunk. It's all over the village. I could hardly get the Cubs to do any work at all on the bonfire for Guy Fawkes night."

"Fiddlesticks."

"Only ten days off. I hope we can get a better Guy this year."

* * *

"Where did this luggage come from, Dad?"

Vic looked at it blearily. He scratched his armpit. The object was strange to him. It was a good stout suitcase of yellowish leather, with brass fittings and a broad strap.

"Mebbe I come by it las' evenin'," he said at last.

Vic opened the suitcase. It was empty. There were red smears on the lining.

He shook his head, then regretted having done so.

Blurred by the fumes of gin and beer there was, however, somewhere in his memory, something about a suitcase. He seemed to feel that it had materialised in the pony-trap, while he was coming home. He had carried it into the shop, and emptied it out onto the slab. There had been, it seemed to Vic, something inside the case, which was now on the slab in the shop.

It was meat.

"Manure," said Vic piously, "like from 'Eaven."

He went out front, on uncertain pins, and into the shop. He could butcher whatever state he was in.

There, sure enough, were two big joints on the slab. They were white meat, fresh. Vic examined them with bleary eyes. The joints seemed like veal. They did not seem *much* like veal, but they seemed more like veal than like anything else Vic could think of.

The meat had come out of that there suitcase. Vic tried to remember where the suitcase had come from. He tried to remember what the meat was, and what he was supposed to do with it.

Looked at one way, the joints seemed to be legs of veal, only not fattening up towards the shoulder like they should. Looked at another way, they seemed more like knuckles of veal, only much longer, going right down to the hoof. Only there wasn't any hoof.

Mrs Mallinson's voice came through the door from the back, like a great baritone blare from a tuba or euphonium: "Remember Mrs Cathcart's order, Father?"

"Of course," said Vic.

It *was* veal, then. It was Mrs Cathcart's veal. He must have come by it last night in Bogham. Ho. Something turned out right, then. Never mind how. He'd think about it when he felt more on top.

They wanted it for stewing. Any bit of a calf you could stew. Some cuts you could roast. Shoulder, loin, best end, fillet or breast, them you could roast. Turn the loin into chops and you could fry it, very tasty. The thought almost made Vic vomit.

These joints were not roasting veal. They were stewing veal, same like Mrs Cathcart wanted.

He skinned and filleted the meat, the two big joints. He thought it must have been a bloody strange calf. But there. They were breeding all kinds these days, anything to fatten them cheaper. Whoever fattened this one, thought Vic, made a proper botch of it. But there. It would feed a dozen at a pinch.

Soon it was all in neat pink slices, piled on the square enamelled tray for the boy to deliver to Mrs Cathcart's. And there was a bit of something beside. Bit of what? Offal? Vic couldn't make it out, rightly. Gin and beer was to blame, same like every Monday. If he'd felt more on top, he'd have known straight away what the bit of meat was. Maybe it was meant for the stockpot? Or to boil up separate with an onion? He put it with the rest, anyhow, as a makeweight. What to do with it was the cook's problem, not his.

* * *

"Arrgh," snarled Albert Monger, crouching on the back doorstep of the Vicarage.

He tugged off his greasy cap, and contorted his degenerate face into a smile.

"Heigh-ho," said the cook absently, memories of her stolen Sunday still filling her mind.

"Oi wunner," mouthed Albert, "c'd Oi 'ave a word wi' the young lady?"

"She's down the garden," sighed the cook.

Mr Robertson had kissed her (oh such a smell of rough cider!) but what were his intentions?

Albert nodded.

He slouched away across the lawn, holding his cap in both blackened hands, looking like an ape dressed by an impoverished showman. He could not afford better clothes. Although criminal by nature, he had not had enough instruction to steal very much, and most of what he did steal was useless. He had sold a few things to Gipsies in Bogham Market – garden tools, carriage lamps, bicycle pumps – but he only had nine shillings in the cottage hidden from his Mam.

He had fallen in love with the Vicarage young lady. He hoped nine shillings would be enough.

Millicent was wearing an old dress for the garden. She was not one to dirty her nice clothes, not dainty Millicent. She had outgrown the old dress; it was very short, and tight over her hips and bust.

She looked up from the rambler rose she was pruning. She saw Albert approaching her, loping crabwise over the lawn with something like a small dead animal in his hands.

She was surprised. The Mongers, mother and son, were considered low by the rest of the village. Nobody talked to them. Millicent had never exchanged a word with either. The Vicar had visited them, of course, for did not Our Lord ennoble the lowest? But he went unhopefully, and came away with a sense of failure, of being followed from the door by indifference and derision.

Albert's lower lip hung wetly from broken and blackened teeth. His eye squinted and his nose dripped. His shoulder was hunched and his legs deformed, owing to malnutrition and ill-treatment throughout childhood. Greasy hair grew low on a receding forehead.

Millicent looked searchingly at his face, her own big blue eyes opening wide like periwinkles in the spring. She saw a look of delinquency and lust, and immediately felt a warm sense of kinship.

In social terms, our Millicent was well equipped to deal with the situation. She had plenty of experience of putting men at their ease (most of them were nothing but big babies). And she was able to use the rambler rose to good effect. She contrived, ever so adroitly, to catch her knitted dress on its thorns. She gave a tiny shriek (like a little girl-bunny caught in a big cruel snare), wriggled her delicious body inside the tight dress, and caught herself on another thorny tendril of the rose-bush.

"Oh fiddlesticks!" she cried, at her most roguish. "I'm all caught up in these horrid, horrid prickles. Could you be ever so sweet, and pull them off?"

"Sure-lee," said Albert, with a retarded but concupiscent leer.

In detaching the thorny sprig from her back, he contrived to rub his elbow against her 'sit-upon', which twitched in response. He was nerving himself to try the same audacious trick in front – but she took the initiative (sometimes a little lady must!) and leaned towards him. He felt, through his ragged sleeve, the soft pressure of her breast.

" 'Ow much yew charge?" he asked hoarsely.

"What did you say, dear?"

"*We* seen 'em, all sorts, Sunnay evenin's. A-creepin' in an' a-creepin' out."

"We?"

"Me an' me Mam."

"Jumping Jehosophat, have you honestly?"

"Ar."

"By the bye, dear, what is your name?"

"Albert, Miss."

"Have you talked to anyone about this, Albert?"

"Sure-lee."

"Who?"

"Me Mam."

"Anyone else?"

"Oi doan talk to nobody else. Leastways, nobody else doan talk to me."

"And your mother?"

" 'Er doan even talk to me, moas-lee."

"I see."

Millicent looked at her new squire speculatively, her 'bee-stung' lip caught in little white teeth made for biting.

She said, "How much money have you got?"

"Noin bob," he said hopefully.

"It's not frightfully much, you know, not for *me*."

"Noa, but see . . ." Albert looked at her slyly. "We'll blab, else."

Millicent made one of her quick decisions. She said, "All right, then. Nine shillings, and you promise not to tell."

"Ar."

"But what about your mother? How can I be sure *she* won't tell anybody?"

"Yew carn't!" Albert laughed. " 'Er doan want no funnin' wi' yew. 'Er want money, 'er dew, for t'keep mum."

"Oh I see." Millicent's brow puckered adorably. She said slowly, "I can't possibly afford to pay blackmail. Besides, I think it's very wrong. But we simply must make sure she keeps her mouth shut."

"Oan'y one way t'dew *that*."

"Yes, dear. That's what we'll have to do, then."

"Ar."

"You don't mind, do you?"

"Noa! 'Er got money 'id some'eres. Oi carn foind un long as she'm sittin' on me arse."

Finding themselves in agreement, they parted the best of friends. Albert loped away in his filthy breeches; Millicent bent with her clippers to the blushing rose.

*   *   *

"Another ramble?" asked the Vicar.

"While it's light. I've been studying ever so hard at those great dusty books, and now Millie needs to fill her lungs with fresh air."

"Tomorrow, don't forget, we are summoned to the hospitable board of Mrs Cathcart."

"In spite of Captain Cathcart going away?"

"She is showing true grit."

"Oh yes. It's frightfully sporting of her, actually, isn't it? Right-ho, then, I'll have an extra strapping hike this evening, for good measure."

*   *   *

"Oi never prop-lee done this," said Albert apologetically, "cep wi' a pig."

"It's just the same, really."

*   *   *

Captain Cathcart's disappearance being yesterday's topic, the Cubs discussed it much less on Tuesday. They reverted to their normal exchanges of ill-informed smut. Major

Martin was able to get the Guy Fawkes bonfire in the playground built a little higher: ever a little higher. There were faggots and brambles cleared from the hedgerows, hazel and birch saplings thinned from the copses, cast-out sticks of furniture collected in a barrow by the Scouts, rotted fence-posts perilous with nails and twists of barbed wire – a grand pile of stuff, a credit to all concerned.

"Bravo, lads," cried Major Martin.

He was in high fettle. Some of the youngest boys had handed over to him small sums in silver they had earned in people's gardens. They had worked weary hours for these sixpences. A few more bob, thought Major Martin, and he could run to another visit to Millicent.

* * *

Mrs Cathcart's cook put the sliced veal in the stewpan with three onions and a bunch of herbs. After a moment's indecision she added the other piece of meat, something restraining her from slicing it. She covered the veal and onions with stock, and simmered them gently for an hour and three quarters on top of the range. When all was tender, or nearly all, she strained the meat and put it in the low oven to keep warm. She made the sauce in a big pan with a handle – butter, flour, two pints of the stock. When it was cooked she added beaten egg-yolks, cream and lemon juice. She brought the sauce almost to the boil again. She would pour it over the meat just before serving, garnished with slices of lemon and sprigs of parsley.

CHAPTER THE FOURTH

In Which One Scarf Encircles Three Necks

Of course Millicent was too young, far too young, to go out to a grown-up dinner party. But Mrs Cathcart had begged that she might be allowed to 'play grown-ups' for just one evening, and after a minute of humming and hawing the Vicar had good-naturedly agreed.

The child looked quite nice, really quite the thing. Everybody agreed that she was quite the young lady. Doctor Bland remarked on how she was growing up. Mrs Bretherton said that it was only to be expected, these days.

Millicent sat at dinner between Doctor Bland and Mr Prynne. Mr Prynne was a new partner in the Bogham lawyers' office; he was a well set up man, whom Mrs Cathcart had decided to 'take up' socially. He had not been to a famous school, but he was a 'Varsity man. Mrs Prynne sat next to the Vicar. She was a little, thin-haired woman with a nervous giggle. Little Millicent (thought Mrs Cathcart) was more self-possessed than Mrs Prynne. There were no giggles from Millicent; there was no conversation either, to be frank, but at least no meaningless titters and shakes of the head and whinnies.

Mrs Cathcart found herself taking a great fancy to Millicent. She felt quite warmly about her. She would take her in hand, she decided, and see if she could make something of her. Now that the Captain was no longer at home, Mrs Cathcart would be lonely, sometimes, and glad of company. They could crochet together, do poker-work and raffia, read to each other, grow fond of each other, grow very, very close to each other . . .

Doctor Bland and Mr Prynne both talked to Millicent. Doctor Bland quite ignored Mrs Cathcart in his efforts to amuse Millicent, and Mr Prynne ignored Miss Dautry on *his* other side. Of course Miss Dautry expected to be ignored. She would not have been asked, except to make up the numbers, and well she knew it. And now the numbers were uneven, because Captain Cathcart was missing. Miss Dautry had Mrs Bretherton on her other side. A 'spare man' had been impossible to find. Doctor Bland and the Vicar were the only 'unattached' gentlemen for miles around – Doctor Bland a widower, and the Vicar, well, better off without, if half what Mrs Cathcart had heard was true. But now the Vicar's little girl was growing up – he could hardly be called a 'spare man' any longer, for the neighbourhood's more fashionable dinner parties.

Apart from Miss Dautry, it was a fine looking party Mrs Cathcart had assembled at her table. All the men (except, of course, the dear Vicar) wore black ties and stiff shirt-fronts and wing collars. Mr Bretherton's collar looked dangerously tight, Doctor Bland's curiously loose. Either the collar had stretched (hardly to be believed – nothing but the best was good enough for Doctor Bland) or his neck had shrunk. It stuck up out of the collar like a vulture's, and like a vulture he bent to talk to Millicent. His voice reverberated round the room, which had rather a low ceiling. He told

Millicent about a horse he had had in 1905, clever as a cat, showed the Master the way across country. Mrs Cathcart thoroughly approved of this conversation. Though dull, it lent tone to the party.

Millicent glanced at the Doctor from time to time, quite composed, eating daintily.

Then they had sole.

"Delicious, delicious," vibrated Mrs Bretherton. "My warmest congratulations, dear Mrs Cathcart, you have a *treasure* in your kitchen."

"Delicious," bleated Miss Dautry, like the echo of a distant sheep. "Treasure."

"Absolutely, absolutely," cried the men, not to be outdone in the courtesies by their lady-folk. "First-rate, top-hole!"

"Abso-jolly-well-lutely," said Mr Bretherton, who was always one to help make any party go.

Mr Bretherton was the bank manager in Bogham. He was, as such, a little bit *touch-and-go*. But he was asked everywhere that Mrs Cathcart was asked, and almost everywhere even that Doctor Bland was asked.

In came the *blanquettes de veau*, tastefully arranged on the biggest of Mrs Cathcart's silver dishes.

"Oh how delicious it does look!" cried Mrs Bretherton, in an ecstasy of admiration, when the dainty confection was offered to her by Agnes the house-parlourmaid. "I can hardly bear, you know," the dimpling creature confided to her hostess, "to break into such an elegant dish."

"Hear hear!" carolled the others.

"I always think veal is so nice," murmured Mrs Prynne, with proper seriousness, to the Vicar, "if it's nice veal."

"A qualification surely needless at this hospitable board,"

said the Vicar with unction, sketching a bow to Mrs Cathcart.

The maid carried the dish round. There was enough, to be sure, but there was no huge surplus. Mrs Cathcart judged the remaining slices with her eye. It had to do nine. Second helpings were bound to be wanted. Mr Bretherton was certain to want a second helping; Doctor Bland also, a notable trencherman for a gentleman of his age; and little Millicent was a growing girl.

Mrs Cathcart took an odd-shaped piece of meat from the centre of the dish, which Cook had artfully hidden, as best she could, with the more normal slices. It was not the piece she really wanted, but she was accustomed to making these sacrifices. It left the greatest number of slices for her guests.

Autumn vegetables joined the veal – broccoli and boiled potatoes.

"Your own, dear Mrs Cathcart?"

"Yes indeed. MacDougall has done wonders."

"I always think," confided Mrs Prynne to the Vicar, "that really fresh vegetables are different, somehow."

"Fresher?" hazarded the Vicar.

"Delicious, delicious," crooned Mrs Bretherton, masticating, with sheerest joy, a tender slice of veal.

"First-rate!"

"Rate," bleated Miss Dautry.

Mrs Cathcart chewed her way doggedly through the piece of meat she had taken. It tasted like veal – as far as the veal had any taste of its own, over onions and herbs and lemon-juice – but its consistency was indubitably curious. Mallinson, however, was to be trusted. He had never sent Mrs Cathcart a bad joint. It was more than his life was worth, and well he knew it. She had all the tradesmen where she wanted them.

Second helpings were accepted with little cries of delighted amazement. Almost everybody had some more! It was quite gratifying for the hostess.

"Our compliments to the cook," said Doctor Bland, in the 'grand manner' that suited him so well.

A chorus seconded this gallant motion.

Mrs Cathcart did not take a second helping, but she set herself to finishing every bit of what she had. It was not in her nature to waste. She chewed indomitably, not displeased by the flavour of the titbit, but puzzled, a little, by a certain rubberiness in its texture.

Mr Prynne murmured in Millicent's ear.

"No secrets!" cried jovial Mr Bretherton.

Doctor Bland was glaring at Mr Prynne.

"Two pounds," said Millicent softly to Mr Prynne.

Mrs Cathcart's sharp ears caught the words.

"Two pounds, Millicent dear?" she asked cozeningly. "And what is costing you such a dreadful lot of money?"

"It is what," said Millicent slowly, raising her wide, blue eyes to Mrs Cathcart, "I should like Father to spend on roses for our little, little garden."

The Vicar looked surprised.

"Two pounds," murmured Mr Prynne. "By Jove. Righty-ho – I'm game!"

Mrs Cathcart chewed and chewed on the last lump of her bit of meat. She got it down in the end, with a sip of *Chablis Superieur*.

* * *

Major Martin went to call at the Vicarage.

Millicent let him in, as she was passing through the hall on her way upstairs; our little heroine was never too proud to perform a 'menial task'.

The cook also heard the bell, and came to the hall to see what was what. (She was a 'cook-general', if truth be told, but she was known in the household as 'Cook'.) The cook arrived in the hall just as Major Martin crossed the threshold, laughing with bonhomie, and tugging off his deer-stalker.

Major Martin winked at Millicent (the rogue), not seeing the pale presence of the cook in the far doorway.

But the cook thought the wink was for her! She was that flustered, she blushed like a raw girl – like the silly-billy she was! She saw herself tempestuously wooed by the Major. After he had rained burning kisses on her upturned face (just as a *start*) he would lead her by the hand into her proper place in Society, as in the books she borrowed from Mrs Cathcart's Agnes, as in *Belinda Below-Stairs*, as in *A Mayfair Cinderella*.

Millicent led Major Martin to the Vicar's den, where that goodly man was doing a newspaper competition.

The Vicar rose courteously. He waved Major Martin to a chair. He was a little nervous of the bluff, gingery warrior (truth to tell), with his martial moustachios. Nor could he altogether approve of the way the Major was taking so much on himself in the village. One or two noses were quite out of joint.

The Major was also uneasy. He felt safe with Millicent, but unsafe with her father, who had a way of using words the Major did not understand.

But the suggestion the Major had come to make was a

good one. He knew it himself: and the Vicar was surely too honest not to recognise the fact. A revolutionary suggestion, true – a cavalier breach with all tradition.

Somewhat hesitant, the Major expounded his idea.

At first the Vicar trembled at the audacity of the scheme! But he came round. He had to!

The Major's suggestion was – a competition in the village for the best Guy! As simple, as daring as that! It would be in two classes, for the under-tens, and the over-tens. Either teams or (haply) individuals would be allowed to enter Guys for the competition. Grown-up help was not to be allowed. The prizes? Why – Major Martin himself would offer one small prize, Mr Melhuish, 'mine host' of The Black Swan, another! The two winning Guys would both go on the bonfire, which was now reaching a satisfactory height.

The Vicar (it went without saying!) was to judge the Guys with, if he thought it best, a committee of two, or of four, assisting him.

"In that way," explained Major Martin, "the judges will be three or five, with your good self. You must have odd numbers, you see."

"Why?" cried the Vicar. The query was forced out of him by very puzzlement.

"Because, with odd numbers, you don't get a tie in the voting."

"Very well thought out," murmured the Vicar wonderingly. "Very perspicaciously analysed. We might, perhaps, venture to enlist the services as judge of Mrs Cathcart, always such a stalwart in the parish. The name of Doctor Bland also leaps to the mind as a possibility."

"Capital suggestions, Vicar!" vouchsafed the Major.

After further discussion (frank, free, and manly) they agreed that the judging would be at tea-time on Guy Fawkes Day itself, on the playground by the church. The winning Guys would then be wheeled in triumph to the bonfire, and hoisted to its summit. The ceremonial 'lucifer' would then ignite the pyre, and the Scouts would start letting off the rockets.

"Champion," said Major Martin.

Thought of the fireworks filled him with joy. The Guides and Brownies had collected thirty-four shillings for them, which had been handed to the Major for safe-keeping. It was far too much. It was criminally extravagant to spend such a sum on fireworks. Dangerous, too. Fourteen shillings was quite enough to spend on fireworks, in a small village.

The Majors 'savings' were mounting up handsomely. Would it be better, he wondered dreamily, to book Millicent for two two-pound sessions, or *one four-pound session*?

* * *

On Sunday the second of November, Millicent went to Early Service at half past seven. More than one eye peeped, a-kindle, between prayerful fingers, when she knelt, so little-girl-submissive, at the altar rail.

At eleven o'clock she went to Matins. She sang in the choir, of course, in a blue surplice which matched her eyes. Under Mrs Cathcart's vigorous handling, the organ threatened to shake loose its pipes.

"Oh ye Whales, and all that move in the waters," sang Millicent, "bless ye the Lord."

The Vicar took as his text the Second Epistle to the

Corinthians, Chapter VI, verses eight and nine: "We are troubled on every side, yet not distressed; we are perplexed, but not in despair; persecuted, but not forsaken; cast down, but not destroyed."

Mrs Cathcart caught Millicent's eye three times during the service. Each time she cast her (it may be believed) a speaking look!

After such devotions in the morning, Millicent was again excused Evensong. This had somehow become customary.

The Vicarage cook was away until late, once again visiting her poor, old mother. Millicent had urged her father to let Cook go.

Millicent entertained Mr Prynne, Major Martin, and Mr Melhuish of The Black Swan, for fifteen minutes each, on the hearth-rug in front of the fire in the Vicar's den. Major Martin had decided on little and often.

Mr Prynne and Mr Melhuish had craftily agreed to 'make things all right' for each other: they were talking business, for all it was Sunday, because both were too busy to make another convenient appointment.

"By Jove, little girl, you're as pretty as paint!" exclaimed Mr Prynne, seeing Millicent in the altogether for the first time.

"Thanks awfully," murmured Millicent, rolling over onto her back on the hearth-rug. "Millie likes being told she's pretty, even if it's nothing but a great big story."

"But I don't, you know," Mr Prynne's manly features grew grave, "much like the idea of you being pawed by those other bounders."

"For six pounds," riposted our heroine, "you can have me all to yourself for three-quarters of an hour."

"That's a bit steep! I'll have to tot up the shekels, what?"

"Are you going to stand there talking all night?"
"No, by Jove, I should just about think not!"

* * *

"Three of 'em agin," cackled old Mrs Monger, peering through the filthy tatters of her curtains. "Yer arst 'er loik Oi said tew?"

"Yer," said Albert. He gave the rehearsed reply in which Millicent had coached him. " 'Er be troyin' t'foind the money."

" 'Er better troy quick, afore Oi blabs."

* * *

Albert reported this sinister exchange to Millicent in the morning.

" 'Er goin' tew make ructions," he said, gesturing with his crooked, receding and pustular chin toward his mother's cottage.

This was his full report – and a sufficient one!

"I'll pop by this evening, dear," said Millicent. "Just when it's beginning to get dark."

* * *

"You run the risk, I fancy, of being benighted," said the Vicar to his 'baby', seeing her dressed up for an evening ramble.

"Father's not to worry," trilled Millicent. "His Millie can see in the dark like a pussy-cat."

He expostulated mildly, but in vain. The tomboy was off,

her Tam o' Shanter perched on her coppery head, something elfin in her expression. She was off to fill, as she expressed it, "Millie's lunglets with sweet fresh air from Heaven".

* * *

Once out of sight of the Vicarage windows, Millicent pulled her 'tammy' down over her ears, so that it quite covered the bright copper of her hair. She crept round to the small, grimy door of the Mongers' cottage. Albert let her in, grinning like a subnormal wolf, his wet lower lip drooping down, and his upper pulled back from black and incomplete teeth. The cast in his eye was exaggerated by the murky dusk.

Millicent kissed him lightly, as soon as they were inside.

"Reckon 'er moight 'ave twenny pund," he whispered.

He drooled with greed.

"Goody gumdrops!" said Millicent.

She kissed him again, fondling the front of his breeches.

Millicent took off her brogues, but kept her woolly gloves on; she had no intention of leaving any fingerprints. She followed Albert up the tiny, rickety staircase, which debouched directly into the single upstairs room. She went silently on stockinged feet; while her swain noisily clumped in the boots he had stolen a month before from the potboy at The Black Swan.

Old Mrs Monger sat by the window, surveying the Vicarage garden. It made Millicent chortle inwardly to think what a surprise the old lady was going to get!

Millicent unwound the long scarf from her little, white neck. It was the Vicar's scarf, striped in yellow and green, awarded him when he made the football team of his Theological College. Millicent was proud to wear it – and he was proud that she should want to wear it. It was the very thing for strangling someone.

Mrs Monger had not looked round, since she thought only Albert had come up the stairs.

Millicent handed one end of the scarf to Albert. Her little hands (stronger than they looked!) kept firm hold of the other end. They put it over the old lady's head, and round her neck, and pulled.

How they pulled!

It was a comical sight. The old lady's chair nearly went over backwards. Millicent gave a little gurgle of laughter, for everything has its funny side, if only you know where to find it.

But even the best of fun must end some time, and soon old Mrs Monger was dead. Millicent wrapped the scarf round her own neck again. They began at once to search for the hidden money. They found it quite soon, under the old lady's bed, in a cardboard box. There were twenty-three pounds in notes, and eight shillings in silver. Millicent took twenty pounds, and gave Albert the rest.

Then she lay back on the bed, and stretched up her arms to him.

CHAPTER THE FIFTH

In Which Creative Effort Gets Its Reward

Young Bobby Tomkins had not made a Guy. There had been no time. It was just his luck that there was a competition this year, when he was so busy, instead of last year, when he had been a little kid of twelve, with nothing to do except make Guys and such.

Willy Melhuish, that bold, bad buccaneer, had shown him what lads did when they got to thirteen. They went off into the woods, and undid their trouser-buttons, and rubbed themselves. All the lads did it all the time, as soon as they were old enough. Some did it in twos and threes, or larger gangs, and some did it by themselves. Willy Melhuish said he got girls to do it for him.

Anyway, it left no time for making Guys for the bonfire, which was a bit of a shame really.

On Tuesday the 4th of November, Bobby bicycled back from the school in Bogham with Muriel Figgis. She was thirteen, like Bobby; a big girl, beginning to get fine jelly-wobbles in front. She had pigtails and a broad face like a cow. Bobby and Muriel were secretly engaged, but nothing had yet come of it.

They were pedalling through Craddock's Wood, when

Muriel suggested looking for blackberries. Bobby knew it was too late for blackberries, but he saw something in Muriel's face, a scheming look, a cowlike excitement, which almost made him fall off his bicycle.

They pulled their machines off the road and into a clump of hazels. Muriel led the way into the wood. Bobby followed, his heart pounding. It was when they were already out of sight of the road that Muriel tripped and fell. Clumsy thing, thought Bobby, just like a girl. She cried but she was not really hurt. They swept the fallen beech-leaves off what she had fallen over. It was a leather suitcase, once smart.

"It'll do to sit on," said Muriel, too dainty to wish to sit on the damp ground.

She sat down on the suitcase. Bobby sat beside her.

"Watcher goin' to do now?" she asked, looking more than ever like a cow in a gym-tunic, looking more than ever sly and inviting.

"Kin I," quavered Bobby, greatly daring, "kin I feel your jelly-wobbles?"

"Through me clothes?"

"No!"

"You'll 'ave to undo me, then."

Bobby undid her! And she let him play with her jelly-wobbles. She began to breathe faster. Then her big, red hand stole down, and began to undo the buttons of his shorts.

"Coo er," she said, peering at what she was holding. "Not much o' this. Do it work? It don't look big enough to work."

" 'Course it works!" cried Bobby, his masculine pride stung.

After a time she said, "Well, it only *jus'* works."

"There's more'n that most times," said Bobby defensively. "But Josh Binks an' me done it dinnertime, an' it 'asn't 'ad time to build up."

"Oo er. I wonder what's in this ole case."

They opened it, and found a severed head wrapped in a piece of sacking.

"Nice hair," said Muriel, smoothing it.

"I b'lieve I reckernise 'im."

"Garn."

"But it's 'ard to tell, when there ain't no rest of 'im. Tell you what, though, it'd make a good 'ead for a Guy."

" 'Ere's a foot," said Muriel, exploring further among the objects in the suitcase.

"What a rotten foot," said Bobby. " 'Is toes is all crooked. We don't what that for the Guy."

"Aw right."

They did up their buttons. Bobby put the head in the saddle-bag of his bicycle, and they rode back to the village.

* * *

The Perkup children had not made a Guy – Queenie, Mabel and Phyllis, shrill and skinny, aged ten, nine and eight, born in wedlock but sired by fathers unknown. Their legal father had been in prison almost continuously throughout their lives, and had never seen any of them. Their mother had narrowly escaped prison for burning down the Vicarage, after the Vicar of the time (the Reverend Gregory Plante) had refused to admit paternity of her eldest child. She had not, however, continued to enjoy such luck, and was now serving a long sentence for cutting off the nose of a fellow prostitute during a brawl in Bogham market.

The children lived with their grandmother. The impoverished squalor of old Mrs Perkup's cottage afforded no materials of any kind for making Guys. In any case they were incapable of making anything. They prowled round the village stealing useless scraps, and tried to assemble them into a Guy. There was a broken perambulator in the nettles of their grandmother's garden, dumped there, as was much other rubbish, by more respectable villagers. The children pushed their rags and sticks into the perambulator, but even Phyllis, the youngest, saw that what they had was a muddle of rags and sticks, not a Guy.

They snivelled apathetically, and gave up.

* * *

" 'Er bin an' gorn all stiff," said Albert to Millicent.

"Has she, darling? Fancy."

Albert, who had readily accepted Millicent's vibrant leadership, asked what he was to do with the corpse of his Mam. Millicent told him to take the body out in the middle of the night, and hide it in a good thick wood.

Carrying Mam turned out to be thoroughly awkward. She had gone stiff while sitting in an upright chair. She went on being an awkward old bitch, Albert thought, even after she was dead. Floppy, she would have been easy to carry, over his shoulder like a sack. Stretched out straight she would have been easy to carry, over his shoulder like a plank. But all bent up double-ways, it was a problem. He finally put her on his head, with her legs sticking up and her own head down his back.

He passed the old witch Perkup's cottage. The garden was a jungle of brambles and nettles, and full of rubbish already. His Mam would be hidden there as well as in the middle of a wood. Albert was tired. He was fed up carrying. His feet hurt, as he had stolen the boots of a man smaller than himself.

Albert dumped his Mam into a clump of nettles at the bottom of the Perkups' garden.

* * *

Bobby and Muriel made a capital Guy, in Muriel's father's woodshed.

They tacked the head they had found securely onto a bit of four-by-four, nailing through loose skin at the neck. Mr Figgis good-humouredly found some old clothes for them, which they pulled over a grain-bag stuffed with straw. A pair of gloves was pinned to the cuffs of Mr Figgis's old Sunday jacket. A pair of ruined boots, bought by Mr Figgis from Horatio Bottomley, dangled at the ends of the trouser-legs. A false beard, made of horsehair stuffing from a mattress which had caught fire, endowed the face with a piratical ferocity which, when it was adorned only by a neat military moustache, it had notably lacked. (Mr Figgis intended, some evening, to dump the mattress in old Mrs Perkup's garden.) A broad-brimmed hat of black cardboard provided the conspiratorial touch proper to the hated 'Gunpowder Plotter'.

"Don't 'e look lifelike?" marvelled Muriel's mother. " 'Ow ever did you make that there face on 'im?"

"Papper matchy," said Bobby. "Learned 'ow at school."

* * *

It was Mabel Perkup who found the ready-make Guy among the nettles at the bottom of the garden. She screamed for Queenie and Phyllis.

(They should all have been at school, but their absence was, perhaps reprehensibly, rather welcomed than otherwise by the schoolteacher, who seldom made any sustained or sincere attempt to enforce their attendance.)

The three little girls looked down at the stiff, shrunken, grotesque, ready-made Guy which Providence had deposited on their doorstep. It was dressed in clothes as ragged and dirty as their own, but more voluminous – rusty black, smeared, dribbled on, spotted, shawl over greasy shawl. Hair of uncertain colour hung lankly each side of a funny face.

The face was funny because the mouth was wide open, with a black tongue sticking out, and the eyes were wide open and bright red. They looked about to pop out, like spat humbugs.

Queenie began issuing commands in a dialect which no adults and few other children would have understood, a version of rural English so debased, like that of slaves on a remote plantation, that it was virtually a foreign language – a tongue with a vocabulary of about twenty words, all obscene.

Jumping to it, Phyllis fetched the broken perambulator, and Mabel went to steal some clothes from her grandmother, who was drunk. Between them they heaved the Guy into the perambulator. It sat up nicely. Queenie painted red circles, the size of apples, on its cheeks, using a lipstick she had stolen from the handbag of a District Visitor. They got a hat from a scarecrow in a new-sown field.

Then they ran out of ideas.

* * *

The Guys were assembling on the playground at four o'clock. The sun was low and red. There was barely another hour of daylight.

"The judging must start punctually and be conducted with despatch," said the Vicar anxiously, "if we are not to be overtaken by the penumbrous shades of eve."

"Indeed," said Mrs Cathcart.

"Used to judge hunters and show hacks," said Doctor Bland. "Never judged a class like this before."

"Who," asked Mrs Cathcart, recoiling with involuntary horror, "are those extraordinary waifs?"

"The Perkup children," the Vicar informed her, a note of disgust creeping into his orotund voice. "I am afraid they represent something of a problem."

"Not a bad Guy, though," said Doctor Bland.

"I would have preferred," said Mrs Cathcart judicially, "a *little* more attempt at realism as to the face. It bears no relation whatever to human features."

"They are very young children," said the Vicar. "One must struggle to make allowances."

"Creditable effort," murmured Doctor Bland. He looked with keen interest at Queenie's depraved ten-year-old face. In five years' time, or three, she would be a little woman worth keeping an eye on. She might be an interesting little person. At least she would be very, very cheap.

A succession of Guys was wheeled up in perambulators and hand-carts. One or two grand Guys trundled up in floats behind ponies or donkeys. The Guys had inept cardboard masks, or heads made of flour-bags.

"Much more lifelike," said Mrs Cathcart.

The Vicar agreed, but Doctor Bland had already decided that the Perkups should have the prize. The eldest one, perhaps in as little as two years . . . And the younger sisters would be twelve or thirteen one day, with the little, infinitely touching beginnings of breasts, with spidery gripping legs and dirty bloomers and infinite gratitude . . . And if they didn't like it, or tried to struggle, he always had plenty of chloroform.

Bobby Tomkins and Muriel Figgis wheeled up their Guy. Bobby was a stalwart of the Boys' Club, and Muriel of the Girls' Sewing Group; they represented the better element in the village; the judges knew their families.

"A fair simulacrum of the human body," said the Vicar, "but they have taken, have they not, scant trouble with the head? The modelling verges on the absurd."

But Mrs Cathcart saw in Muriel's cow-like eye a look which combined wordless, passionate appeal with half-formulated yearnings. With proper handling, thought Mrs Cathcart, something could be made of young Muriel. She was already developing on lines Mrs Cathcart admired.

The Perkups' Guy was 'short-listed' among four for the Under-Tens class, and Bobby's and Muriel's among five for the Over-Tens.

Doctor Bland went to have a closer look at the Perkup children's effort. It was, to be sure (he admitted to himself), grotesquely unrealistic, a botched job, a pathetic attempt at the likeness of a person. But the little tattered savages with the shifty, criminal eyes, set his heart thudding in his susceptible breast. He prodded the Guy absently, concluding that it was a bundle of sticks wrapped in rags from the rubbish dump. Either the Guy or the children – perhaps both – gave off an acrid, septic odour; Doctor Bland inhaled it with a connoisseur's delight.

He had a word with Queenie about her Guy, patting, the while, her undernourished shoulder. He could not understand her reply.

Mrs Cathcart inspected Bobby's and Muriel's Guy. Drawing Muriel aside she asked her, ever so casually, if the child would like special embroidery lessons, since she showed such promise in the Sewing Group? Muriel replied obliquely that things depended. It would be nice, she said, to win the prize for the best Guy.

Mrs Cathcart understood. She fingered, almost caressingly, the Guy's ridiculous features, half hidden under the opulent horsehair beard. The 'face' (to dignify it by an epithet which it scarcely, in honesty, deserved) was oddly flaccid to the touch. Mrs Cathcart, whose mind was on "special embroidery lessons" in the cushioned privacy of her morning-room, vaguely assumed that the head was made of a half-inflated football bladder.

The arguments of the judges verged on the acrimonious. But the Vicar was at last overruled by the superior determination of his colleagues.

The Under-Tens prize was awarded to the Perkup children – half a crown and a box of chocolates. The Over-Tens prize was accepted by Muriel on behalf of Bobby and herself – five shillings (munificent Mr Melhuish!) and a box of chocolates.

There was widespread disagreement, freely voiced, with

the findings of the judges. The parents of unsuccessful children went away in dudgeon, leaving only a rump to watch bonfire and fireworks.

The winning Guys were wheeled to Major Martin's bonfire.

CHAPTER THE SIXTH

In Which A Medical Man Is Undone

It had been one of the fine warm spells which sometimes make the English autumn glorious. The wood of the bonfire was therefore beautifully dry, and it went up spectacularly. Major Martin and his Cubs deserved the greatest credit. There were "oohs" and "ahs" from the few villagers who had stayed to watch the bonfire. The heat was tremendous; everyone backed away. The flames licked at the two winning Guys high on the blazing faggots.

The Scouts, under the military direction of Major Martin, began to let off the fireworks. The display was somewhat disappointing, owing to the small number of fireworks purchased.

* * *

"I say," said Millicent, watching from her bedroom window. "What a putrid little beast of a firework display."

Even as she spoke these petulant words, however, the very best of the rockets exploded into golden rain not far from her window. A feverish glare briefly illuminated her breasts, though not (it was to be hoped) sufficiently for them to be seen by those round the bonfire. Reminded of the adorable things, which were still something of a novelty to her, she stroked them, murmuring endearments.

"Ar," said Albert, who was beginning to overcome his bashfulness at being seen naked by Millicent.

"What is it, dear heart?" asked Millicent absently, watching the 'squibs' and 'Catherine wheels' in the playground.

Albert intimated, with a series of wet animal grunts, that he was anxious to enjoy his pert friend's favours.

"Of course," said Millicent, always game. "But I feel I must stay here and watch the fireworks. Out of loyalty, you know. Still, there's no need to waste time."

"Ar?"

"Come on, juggins! You're not here to pose for your picture, you know!"

"Oi'm better fronty-ways."

"I daresay you are, sweetest, but if I turn round I can't watch the fireworks. Do get on, we haven't got all night, you know."

"Oi doan roightly know 'ow, Miss."

"Just think of me as a pig."

* * *

The champion Under-Tens Guy, the Perkup children's Guy, was the first to start burning properly. Flames ran up its comical old travesty of a gown, and hissed in the greasy 'hair'. Its brittle rigidity began to desert it. It sagged from the rope round its 'waist' until it hung, bent double, in the flames.

The Over-Tens champion, Bobby's and Muriel's Guy,

was not slow to follow. Not it! Amid ragged cheers, its straw-filled torso began to crackle.

* * *

"Ooh," cried Millicent, watching agog in her bedroom window. To Albert she added, "That was lovely, dear heart, you are clever, but it wasn't exactly what I expected."

"Yew say dew un loik the ole pig."

"Yes, precious, but I didn't expect you to take me quite so literally. Still, Father says the day you don't try something new is the day you begin to die."

* * *

The rope round the waist of the Perkup children's Guy burned through and parted. The little Guy, itself now crackling merrily, tumbled down the side of the bonfire. It rolled a few feet and lay sizzling on the grass.

The Perkup children, eating their prize chocolates, screamed at each other words which, fortunately, few of those present understood.

The Vicar was wearing his striped College football scarf, 'borrowed back' from his tomboy daughter. It showed that he was a man of action, as well as of prayer, and now was his chance to confirm it! With a cheerful laugh he darted forward with a stick to push the Guy back onto the fire.

He paused, puzzled. A smell of roasting meat impinged on his fastidious nostrils. He could not at first account for it. The roasting of a whole ox had, in the 'olden days', been a tradition of the village. But those days were long gone: no ox caused this persistent and delightful smell of roasting.

"What can be cooking?" asked Mrs Cathcart, whose own high-bridged nose was a-wrinkle with the appetising aroma.

"Ole dog crawled into the fire, mebbe," hazarded Mr Figgis.

The Vicar looked grave. "Dogs," he said, "are not allowed on the playground, because . . ."

He glanced at Mrs Cathcart, and forebore, from delicacy, to explain the hygienic motive which had occasioned this necessary rule.

Mr Figgis, who was wearing big rubber boots, thrust a foot under the smouldering remnants of the Perkup children's Guy. He heaved it into the incandescent heart of the bonfire, where it burst into pleasing flame again.

Mrs Cathcart nodded approvingly. She was tidy herself, rigorously so, and approved of tidiness in others. Like father, like daughter, it was to be hoped. If little Muriel was a tidy soul, her visits to Mrs Cathcart would be doubly satisfactory.

Mrs Cathcart, overheated by the fire, allowed herself to daydream for a moment about these promised visits. The servants would be told *not* to disturb them . . .

Muriel's Guy, meanwhile (hers and Bobby's, really, but Mrs Cathcart found herself thinking of it as Muriel's) was nodding its head in a curious fashion. Much of its straw and sacking body was already consumed, and the flames were rushing up the gallant horsehair beard. It appeared that the head was not securely fixed to the wooden neck. From nodding, it flopped completely forward, dangled for a few seconds, and then fell! It bounced down to the ground, and rolled like a football towards the eager watchers.

"Your job again, Mr Figgis!" cried Mrs Cathcart jovially, for she felt warmly disposed towards the whole family.

"That's the ticket," agreed the Vicar. "Score a goal, Mr Figgis!"

Mr Figgis laughed. Recalling the prowess of his schooldays, he let fly with a massive boot, connected solidly, and sent the 'ball' soaring skywards! But the strength of his kick was superior to its direction. Instead of 'scoring a goal' in the midst of the fire, it landed amongst a group of laughing folk!

Though smouldering, it did not, by lucky chance, set fire to cloak or Ulster. No harm was done. Innocent merriment was all that the accident provoked.

" 'Ere you are, then," called a strapping villager, and booted the 'ball' back to Mr Figgis.

Landing a little short of its intended target, the 'ball' rolled invitingly towards the Vicar. As capable (as witness the glorious scarf!) of manly sports as any of them, he, too, let loose with a hearty kick. But, to his chagrin, the 'ball' sped towards Mrs Cathcart!

Not a whit abashed was she. Booted also (no dainty pumps for Mrs Cathcart when bonfires were toward), she kicked as heartily as any of them!

And so an impromptu game took place, long remembered in the village. And what shrieks of glee there were, what helpless bursts of laughter! It was the grandest fun. Champion of them all, unquestioned, was Mrs Cathcart. How she dribbled and shot the ball. The men-folk were loud in their acclaim.

"Never played much footer," she said at last, rosy and panting, to the Vicar. "Hockey and lacrosse were my games!"

* * *

"Father will be back in a minute," said Millicent, seeing that the bonfire was burning low, and that people were beginning to drift away to their high teas.

"Oi be goin'."

"Not for a sec. There's time for another, if you look sharp."

"Oi carnt. 'Er be all floppity."

"You are a wash-out! Is that better? Is *that* better? Is Millie's little friend going to be a good boy?"

"Ow. Ow ow ow."

"No, not very good."

* * *

It was reported to Doctor Bland that there had been no sign, for several days, of old Mrs Monger.

"She is not on my list," said Doctor Bland austerely. "Heaven forbid. Have a word with Doctor Corbishley."

For the good doctor knew that his junior colleague, one of the 'new school', was full of socialistic notions of 'duty'. Though in some ways an embarrassment to Doctor Bland – in regard, for example, to his accent, his clothes, his poverty – he was a useful partner, as he willingly took, on his narrow shoulders, the tasks which Doctor Bland was too fastidious to perform.

Within a week, then, Doctor Corbishley hurried round to the Mongers' cottage.

Albert, lip drooping and eye askew, opened the door a crack and refused to open it any wider. Two strong men stood face to face, inches apart. Doctor Corbishley's suspicions were aroused. He smelt something 'fishy', above and beyond the indescribable smell of Albert's breath.

Albert said his Mam had gone away to stay with her sister. After much coaching by Millicent, he was word-perfect in this story, which, being but ten words long, represented the limit of the strain to which his memory could be subjected.

"Where does your mother's sister live?" Doctor Corbishley asked keenly.

Albert looked at him blankly. He had no answer to this question. Millicent had not told him what to say.

"Me Mam," Albert repeated doggedly, " 'er gone 'way t'stop at 'er sister's."

Not another word could Doctor Corbishley get out of him.

* * *

"I smell a rat," reported Doctor Corbishley to Doctor Bland.

"If that's all you smell, in that hovel," said Doctor Bland, with fine disdain and a touch of patrician wit, "you can count yourself damned lucky."

* * *

Albert reported, a-dither, to his Millie. She soothed and heartened him (Eve's role, throughout history!) with a caressing little hand.

"Oo er," said Albert, gasping.

"Gracious," said Millicent, withdrawing her hand. "What a waste."

* * *

Doctor Corbishley asked shrewd questions amongst his patients. None knew of any sister of old Mrs Monger's. None had seen her depart from her cottage, on foot or by any other conveyance. Her face had not been seen at the windows of the cottage, nor her voice, hoarsely blasphemous, heard through the cracks in the walls.

"It's a curious business," confided Doctor Corbishley to his sister. "When all's said and done, one can't help wondering . . ."

"That's right, dear," said Edwina.

So Doctor Corbishley returned to the assault, like the doughty campaigner he was.

But whose pert face should he see, peeping through the half-open door of the Mongers' cottage, but Millicent's!

"Great Scott," he vouchsafed.

"I thought it my duty to look in," explained Millicent. "Mrs Monger has gone away to stay with her sister, you see, and young Monger is such a hopeless duffer at looking after himself! I daresay you'd be the same! I always think men are nothing but big babies."

"Can I come in?"

"Everything is ever such a muddle. I was just going to try to get things shipshape."

Doctor Corbishley felt inspired, elated, by the little thing's unselfishness. He followed her gladly into the reeking darkness of the single downstairs room.

"Where is the son?" he asked.

"Working, I expect," quoth Millicent.

The smell of putrefying fragments of food was mingled with that of vermin, both with the odour of bodies unwashed from birth and of their unspeakable clothes, of decay and rot, and of primitive 'sanitation'. Cockroaches could be imagined, perhaps heard, rustling across the spongy floor; a rat, unmistakable even in the gloom, scampered fatly along the bottom of a sweating wall.

Millicent shrieked! She clutched at Doctor Corbishley. He put an arm about her, protective, gallant!

She seemed almost to swoon.

"Upstairs," she murmured, "there is a kind of bed. If I could lie down for half a jiffy . . ."

"Of course!" cried her cavalier.

He helped her cautiously up the perilous little stairs. She leaned on him heavily.

Sighing, she stretched herself, on her back, on the narrow couch.

"Hold me," she said, in a tiny, frightened voice.

No second bidding, be sure, needed he!

"So tight," whispered Millicent, "my blouse."

"Let me, dear . . ."

"Ooh Doctor, an examination of Millie's toys?"

"Yum yum," mumbled the rogue ecstatically. "Better, dear? A little calmer?"

"Gracious," said Millicent, her fingers busy with his buttons. "What a great big *man* . . . Why is he hiding? Doesn't he want to say how-d'you-do to Millie? Yes, he *does* . . ."

"Not so bloody big," said Albert critically, as he emerged from the noisome darkness of a corner. "Yew want Oi brain 'im, Miss?"

"Help, help," cried Millicent. "No, don't do that, Albert. I will go and speak to Doctor Bland about this dreadful assault."

"For pity's sake," wailed the hapless victim of Millicent's artful trap.

"Well, then," she said kindly, "perhaps I will take pity on you. Mrs Monger *is* staying with her sister, isn't she?"

"Yes!" cried Doctor Corbishley.

"Sure?"

"Yes!"

"That's a good boy. Have you got two pounds, dear?"

"No."

"Then do up your trousers, you naughty man."

* * *

Muriel Figgis was being difficult.

Sometimes she said she had too much homework. Sometimes she said she had to help her mother with the new net curtains. Sometimes she had to stay in to look after her little brother and sister. Excuse followed excuse.

But Mrs Cathcart was not going to give up. A bargain, according to her 'code', was a bargain!

Meanwhile Millicent came to tea – the very first time she was asked!

"The servants are both *out*, dear," said Mrs Cathcart when Millicent arrived. "They have the afternoon off every Thursday, and go, I believe, all the way to Bogham, in the motor-bus."

"Shall I get the tea, then, Mrs Cathcart," piped eager Millicent.

"We will both get the tea, dear, together."

"Right-ho!"

Mrs Cathcart was ever so gentle and patient with Millicent. She did not want to frighten the little thing. (With

Muriel Figgis her tactics could, she thought, be more direct – if she ever got the tantalising imp into her house!) But, oh! how artful Mrs Cathcart was. Oh how clever! She said she had, upstairs in her bedroom, some clothes she did not want. Far too young for her, she simpered. Would Millicent care to try some of them on?

"Ooh," cried Millicent, "how simply, simply lovely, how frightfully kind of you, how too gallumptious for words!"

Well, of course, to try on a dress – you must first *take off* the dress you have on!

"What a big girl she's growing," crooned Mrs Cathcart. "Two! One on each side! I wonder which one is prettier? May Mrs Cathcart see? May Mrs Cathcart . . . touch?"

* * *

"Next Thursday," said Millicent.

"Ar," said Albert. He looked frightened.

"The servants will be out. I'll keep the old woman out of the way. That will be frightfully easy. She likes prodding. Aren't people funny? There's a jewel-case on the table in her bedroom, and a lot of silver in the sideboard in the dining-room."

CHAPTER THE SEVENTH

In Which
A Lady Loses Her Treasures

Cook, at the Vicarage, sighed with discontented longings. Her Sunday had been a disappointment. Mr Robertson had kissed her again, but he had been too shy or too careful to do anything else. And Cook wanted ever so much more! It was a girl's birthright. Agnes at Mrs Cathcart's said so. "It's a girl's birthright," said Agnes, 'an' if you never felt it you been deprived."

"Felt what?" quavered Cook, torn between fascination and terror.

"Thrustin'," said Agnes obscurely. "But if you 'old on to 'is dingle-dangles, 'e can't do nothin' you don't give your consent to."

But it had not reached that stage with Mr Robertson.

And there had been no further move from Major Martin! None!

Cook put on her hat and stepped out moodily towards Mallinson's to talk about a joint for Wednesday. A walk, she thought, would get her out of the house and stop her moping. She was a female (all female!) of thirty-five, with legs like trees and an immense pelvis. She walked with a roll, like a sailor-man. He face was sallow, and resembled suet. Her moustache was only visible in a good light.

She skirted the playground by the church, where the remnants of the bonfire made a large black eyesore. Major Martin had made the fire! Oh oh, thought Cook, picturing his dingle-dangles with a feeling of sick excitement. She passed the gate into Mrs Cathcart's forbidding garden, and approached Mallinson's. Opposite was Columbine Cottage, where Major Martin lived! Oh oh! Perhaps she would glimpse him! If he should wink at her again, she could not answer for her self-control, she was that weak, that susceptible!

The front door of Columbine Cottage opened as she passed the gate. Cook's heart pounded! But it was Mrs Martin who came out, dressed in a purple coat, ever so posh.

Mrs Martin called back over her shoulder, "You find that money or I'm off to the police. Don't think I don't mean it."

A kind of groan answered her.

Mrs Martin slammed the front door shut. The whole cottage seemed to shake. It did not look a very strong cottage. Mrs Martin's face was red with anger; it was almost the colour of her coat. She hurried along the garden path and through the little wicket gate. She was walking blindly, not seeing Cook at all, seemingly, though she almost brushed against her. Her heels went away tock-tock-tock along the road past Mallinson's.

Another groan came from Columbine Cottage, clearly audible in the quiet road.

Cook was seized by a mad resolve!

She glanced round. There was no one in sight. No face

watched her from Mallinson's windows. The road was deserted.

A third groan, heartbreaking, issued from the cottage, which was quite newly built, in the Tudor style, and had thin walls and ill-fitting windows.

It seemed to Cook a cry from the heart – a cry to *her* heart! Was she made of stone, that she could resist so passionate an appeal for help, for comfort?

"I come to thee!" murmured Cook, and sped like a bird to the varnished door of Columbine Cottage.

The door was not locked!

Palpitating, Cook slipped inside!

* * *

Dolly Martin was not angry that Ernest had stolen the Scouts' money. After all, her own Dads was a wholesale grocer, a business man. Dolly had been brought up to regard a legitimate profit as a sign of good sense, of solid citizenship. Anything you could get away with, in a genteel way, was fair pickings. If Dads had run the Boy Scouts, he wouldn't have lost by it, not Dads. But for Ernest to *keep it from her* – that was what made Dolly see red. To keep it from her, who paid all the bills with what Dads gave her, and spend it on some girl.

Girls, thought Dolly bitterly. She'd girl them.

So she went to the Post Office to write an anonymous letter to the police, accusing Major Martin of stealing the Scouts' money.

* * *

Major Martin sat in 'his' chair in the sitting-room of Columbine Cottage. A cigarette smouldered, forgotten, on an ashtray by his feet. He held his head in his hands and rested his elbows on his knees.

Dolly was turning nasty.

Actually that was inaccurate. She had been nasty all along. Major Martin had begun by disliking her mildly, but by now he disliked her intensely. What he liked was her money. He liked anybody's money, but she, or her gargoyle of a father, had more than most. They had been quite pleased to hand some of it over to him.

And now, all because of a few bob borrowed from the Scouts, Dolly was saying all kinds of bloody offensive things to him. She used words Major Martin didn't know she knew. She threatened to cut off his allowance – the few quid that enabled him to buy a smoke and run the two-seater and have a beer with Tom Melhuish at The Black Swan.

It was unfair.

"It's not fair," groaned Major Martin, wondering how he could get through life without beer and fags and the old bus.

And Millicent. Of course Dolly's pittance didn't run to Millicent. That was why he had to borrow from the Scouts. Anybody who was fairminded could see he was *compelled* to borrow from the Scouts.

"Not my fault at all," Major Martin groaned.

A kind of cough interrupted his bitter and self-pitying reverie.

He looked up.

To his great astonishment, a female he dimly recognised, but could not put a name to, stood in the doorway of the sitting-room, nearly filling it, with a ghastly simpering expression on her disgusting face. She was about the Major's own age, a fright, a hideous woman, a damned intruder, a loathesome sight.

He recognised her as the Vicarage cook, with whom he had never exchanged a word. She was always out when he went to see Millicent.

The Major was quite nettled that a bloody slavey should have the infernal gall to come bursting in on him while he was sitting having a groan. If a fellow couldn't sit and groan in his own house without other people's servants crashing in on him, things, thought the Major, had come to a pretty pass.

"Get out," he said.

The creature made a frightful grimace with her filthy mouth. Nervous terror suddenly gripped the Major's bowels. The woman was mad. She was a dangerous lunatic. She was big and strong. Would she strangle? Stab? Major Martin was – always had been – the most abject of physical cowards, and of the very few threats to his safety which he had ever faced, in a lifetime of avoiding such things, this was easily the most alarming.

"Get out, you bloody old bitch," screamed Major Martin, his voice shrill with abject terror. Then he added, whimpering (for he was the soul of courtesy), "Please."

* * *

Dolly Martin gripped a pencil in her left hand, so as to disguise her writing. On a piece of scrap paper she laboriously wrote:

'The Boy Scouts have been swindled by Maj Martin. They collected lots of money which he has stolen. Ask to see his

Accounts. Ask what he spent the money on. You will find he 'as stole seven pounds, maybe 8 or 10.

'A friend.'

She put this artful missive into an envelope, addressed the envelope (using her left hand) to P.C. Flockett, at the Police Station, which was a room of his mother's cottage, and stuck a stamp on it.

She popped the letter into the pillar box outside the Post Office.

* * *

Cook was dumbfounded.

She opened her mouth to say something, but the devil had run away with her tongue. Nothing came out of her mouth at all, except a little, high, wailing noise.

Major Martin screamed at her again.

Cook could hardly take in what he said, she was in that much of a dither. Was he beside himself with animal passion? Surely that must be it. Agnes at Mrs Cathcart's said all men gave in to animal passion if you gave them half a chance. Mr Robertson didn't, but Major Martin was a fish of another colour. He was beside himself with beastly lust, that was what it was. Cook felt that she, too, was beside herself with beastly lust.

But was this lustful animal the debonair, self-possessed gentleman who had given her a wink? Yes, he was! No doubt of it. That was the funny part. It was all quite a puzzle to Cook.

Major Martin stood up.

Cook saw that he was trembling. Yes, really and truly trembling. His knees were almost knocking together, and his hands were shaking like leaves. He was in the grip of a veritable tempest of passion.

Cook was, too!

This was the moment she had been waiting for.

He would not actually shower burning kisses on her upturned face, not unless she squatted down, seeing she was a good bit taller than him, but he could shower burning kisses on her downturned face. It was all one to Cook. She thought burning kisses could shower just as well upwards as downwards.

Even in her wild excitement, she remembered Agnes' advice: "Get a good 'old of them dingle-dangles, dear, you'll find they fit the 'and like a bell-rope."

Resolving to grip *and tug*, Cook closed her eyes ecstatically.

There was a strangled sob.

Passionate boy!

There was a shuffling, rustling noise. Could it be? It must be . . . His trousers!

Agog with curiosity to see her fate, Cook opened her eyes. She looked blankly across the room. It was empty, Major Martin had gone. She felt utter disbelief.

But where had he gone? Where but – the bedroom!

Cook launched herself at the stairs and thundered up them.

* * *

Dolly Martin strode back towards Columbine Cottage, her mood a great deal more cheerful. The rush of blood to her head, which had made her feel quite giddy, had dispersed itself when she wrote and posted the letter to the police.

They'd catch him and she wouldn't lift a finger. Anything they wanted to know, she'd tell them. A wife couldn't be compelled to give evidence against her husband: but there wouldn't be any compulsion about it.

She pictured herself in the witness box: "Yes, My Lord, but I put my duty to my country higher than what I do my duty to my mate." In black, sort of mourning, dignified yet touching.

* * *

The bedroom door locked against the madwoman, Major Martin felt almost safe. His heart thudded painfully against his ribs, his throat was dry, his breath rasped harshly. A damned narrow squeak.

He heard massive footsteps pounding up the stairs and along the little passage. Great fists beat on the door.

Oh God, was it strong enough?

It creaked. It would splinter, shatter. Huge hands would fasten round his neck.

Major Martin fell to his knees, blubbering with terror.

The banging continued. The doorknob was twisted and rattled. A wailing noise could be heard. The door was strong enough! From the bottom of his manly heart, Major Martin blessed the honest English workman who had made the door.

On the full tide of his joyful relief, another thought struck him. Dolly might come back and find the woman here! The woman would kill Dolly!

"Please God," prayed the Major, "let her kill Dolly."

* * *

Cook saw what it was. Her boy was bashful! Agnes said it sometimes happened.

She peeped through the keyhole. After twenty years in domestic service, there wasn't a keyhold made she couldn't peep through.

He was on his knees. Yes he was. Praying!

Cook had quite enough of that sort of thing, living in the Vicarage. Prayers had their place in life, no doubt of that, but they didn't go with grabbing a gentleman's dingle-dangles. There was a time for the one and a time for the other, but you couldn't be doing them both at once.

At least, Cook thought not. Agnes might know.

Cook retraced her steps, in something of a daze, and plodded sadly downstairs. It all seemed as far away as ever.

* * *

As Dolly Martin approached her home, a woman came out of the front door. Dolly recognised the Vicar's cook. She was in a dream, a proper daze. She didn't hardly know where she was going.

So that was who it was. Rage filled Dolly again. Not a girl at all, which you might have understood, but this great camel of a woman, this ugly great cow of a woman, smelling of cabbage, this common creature.

And doing it in Dolly's own house! Under a roof she had paid for, in a bed she had paid for, between sheets she had paid for . . . Or did they do it on top, all uncovered?

Oh! said Dolly to herself, feeling quite ill with anger.

She went back to the Post Office to write another anonymous letter to the police. She posted the new one to the Inspector in Bogham.

* * *

Thursday was a nasty, wet day with a cold, gusty wind. But merry Millicent was not one to be put off by a drop of rain. In thickest shoes, and Father's great big mackintosh, she set off with a laugh to Mrs Cathcart's.

There was to be another trying-on session of Mrs Cathcart's cast off clothes, in front of the morning-room fire. And the servants were out, all afternoon, till late!

Albert, watching, saw her go. He ran out of his own cottage – soaked through at once in his skimpy, stolen clothes – and loped behind her to Mrs Cathcart's.

She turned once, briefly, to make sure he was there.

* * *

"These, dear child," crooned Mrs Cathcart, "are evening bloomers! Apricot coloured, and the purest silk!"

"Ooh," said Millicent, standing shyly in her 'shift'. "How simply lovely."

"Shall we try them on, dear? Oh no, dearest one, fie, for shame! Not my pretty silk over your flannel, darling. The naughty great flannel must come off first, mustn't it? Shall Mrs Cathcart help? By pulling here, and pulling here . . . Oh my, oh my, what a grown up lady, my woolly bear, my grizzly bear . . ."

The enraptured lady buried her face in what she called her 'secret garden', giving Millicent a sensation more (perhaps) surprising than pleasant.

Millicent, listening intently, heard the chink of silver candlestick on candlestick. She frowned for a second. But her hostess was quite preoccupied.

* * *

Mrs Cathcart's house-parlourmaid and cook came back to find the house in some disturbance. All the silver was missing from the sideboard in the dining-room, and the mistress's bedroom was enough to make a person cry! All the drawers emptied, clothes flung everywhere, the jewels gone, mud all over the floor from the robber's boots.

The mistress had heard nothing. Her bosom was heaving, her cheeks were unnaturally pink, her eyes seemed to shine with inner visions. Miss Millicent had left a little while before.

Mrs Cathcart was upset to find that everything of value she possessed had been stolen.

* * *

"Ripping!" said Millicent, calling in at Albert's cottage on her way home. "I'll take these small things. You look after the silver. I'll find out how to sell it in a day or two. I don't suppose you wore gloves, did you, dearest? No. What an old silly you are. Your fingerprints will be all over the house, won't they? So you must remember to be very good, and do just what Millie tells you, and be satisfied with whatever Millie decides to give you. I was with Mrs Cathcart all the time, wasn't I, precious? Every moment I was in the house."

* * *

P.C. Lockett arrived the minute he had finished his high tea. Mrs Cathcart was almost prostrate at the loss of all her treasures. P.C. Lockett was able to deduce, from the clues his trained eye observed, that someone had come into the house from outside (leaving mud here and there) and stolen the things.

The Constable used Mrs Cathcart's telephone to get through to the Station in Bogham. The Inspector came out in a big black car. He confirmed P.C. Lockett's conclusions, praising that conscientious officer for the accuracy of the deductions he had drawn.

By this time – it was nearly midnight – Mrs Cathcart was sufficiently mistress of herself to answer questions.

"No one," she told the Inspector, dabbing still at her eyes with the corner of an oh-so-tiny scrap of handkerchief, "knew where I kept my pretty things, my little baubles."

"Your husband . . ." hazarded the Inspector.

She silenced him with a speaking look.

"The servants?" he enquired, pursuing a new line of interrogation.

"They, of course, knew. But it was they who discovered the outrage."

"So they *say*, ma'am."

The cook and the house-parlourmaid were thereupon arrested and taken to the cells in Bogham.

CHAPTER THE EIGHTH

In Which Much Business Is Transacted

P.C. Lockett had been excited and exhausted by the events of Thursday night. He was not in the mood for a letter on Friday morning. Also, he had somehow, in the confusion of Mrs Cathcart's house, and the intoxication of the Inspector's praise, mislaid his reading glasses.

His mother was no help. She had never fancied reading.

The letter looked unimportant – an illiterate scrawl, in pencil, on a cheap envelope – but P.C. Lockett knew his duty. He went next door to Mr Tomkins, to get the letter read to him.

"Young Bobby's the scholard," said Mr Tomkins, who was sub-Postmaster as well as 'Newsagent and Confectioner'.

Bobby, just off to school, read the letter aloud, with some difficulty. His voice was in the process of breaking. Some words came out in a piping treble; some, unpredictably, in profoundest bass. He gave, in consequence, a curious zigzag impression of the letter.

But its ominous import was clear.

"Fancy," said Mrs Tomkins, who was eating a pork

chop. "Those poor little childer collected all that money, and that nasty Major Martin stole it."

"Drank it all at The Black Swan, likely," said Mr Tomkins.

"Or give it to that Mrs Martin," said Mrs Tomkins sourly, her voice muffled by a mouthful of fried potatoes, "*as* she calls 'erself. Airs an' graces, but she's not a proper lady to my way of thinkin', not like Mrs Cathcart or that Miss Millicent, bless 'er pretty face, same like a flower I often say."

"Lumme, what a Go," said P.C. Lockett.

He returned unhappily to his mother's cottage, wondering how he could inspect Major Martin's Scout accounts without his reading glasses.

He was met by a telephone call from the Inspector in Bogham (for police efficiency required that he, too, was on the 'instrument'.)

"Bad business," said the Inspector, who had received a letter like P.C. Flockett's. "Can't ignore it. Serious charge. Misappropriation. Go and face the man Martin with the evidence, and watch his reaction."

"Ar," said P.C. Lockett. He hoped he could watch a reaction without his reading glasses.

He decided to go along later in the morning, when he had had time to digest his breakfast.

* * *

Bobby Tomkins told Muriel Figgis about the letter, as they bicycled to school together. He swore her to secrecy on a blood-curdling oath. She told thirty-seven girls and four teachers within a few minutes of her arrival at school. Bobby told two dozen boys during the morning.

There was widespread disapproval in the school of the Major's theft of the money.

* * *

Mrs Tomkins went out for a stroll in the middle of the morning, which took in all the shops in the village and a fair number of cottages. She finished at Mallinson's. She did not want any meat, but she wanted to tell the Mallinsons about the letter.

The Mallinsons had already heard. Several people had been to the Post Office, and had been given the facts by Mr Tomkins.

"A tittle-tattle, that's what 'e is," said Mrs Tomkins, with deep disapproval of her spouse. " 'Ighly confidential letter to the police, an' 'e 'as to tell everybody."

They all looked across the road at Columbine Cottage.

Mrs Martin came out in her posh, purple coat.

"That's new, I declare," said Mrs Mallinson in her voice of brass. "That there coat."

"Ar. Never seen that afore," concurred her mate.

"So that's where the pore little childer's money been an' gone," said Mrs Tomkins.

"That's it," agreed her hearers.

* * *

Dolly Martin stepped out to do her shopping with a high heart. Dads had sent the new installment of her allowance. She could buy whatever she liked the look of, without a worry in the world, especially now that she wasn't going to give Ernest another penny piece.

"Morning, Mrs Tomkins," she called to that worthy dame, who was coming out of Mallinson's. Her tone had that democratic heartiness which has ever marked the manners of Merrie England.

But Mrs Tomkins turned away with a face of stone, and waddled back towards the Post Office.

And so it was everywhere, all over the village, all morning.

* * *

"I 'ave to require a hanswer to the hallegations contained 'erein," enunciated P.C. Flockett, in proper form, to Major Martin. "Bein' hinstructed thereto by my superior hofficer, 'avin' reference to the Hinspector."

"Oh God," said Major Martin.

He surprised P.C. Flockett by bursting into tears.

P.C. Flockett, nonplussed, went back to his mother's cottage to telephone for further instructions. He had observed a reaction, but he did not know how to interpret it.

But they said at the Station that the Inspector was busy, and could not be interrupted.

* * *

The Inspector was busy interrogating his suspects.

Mrs Cathcart's cook and house-parlourmaid were accustomed to return to the village from Bogham by the six o'clock motor bus, after their regular Thursday afternoon out. But on the previous afternoon they had broken with precedent – they had accepted the offer of a 'lift' from a gentleman with a motor. So they said! They did not know the gentleman's name. They did not, forsooth, know the make of his car. They had not made a note of the number of the car – deeply suspicious circumstance! The gentleman, they said, was a 'commercial' – he travelled in elastics, surgical stockings, and rubber 'sundries'. They did not know the name of the company that employed him. They did not know, to a minute, how long the journey took, nor at what exact hour they returned home to Mrs Cathcart's.

"Tell me more about this 'gentleman'," persisted the Inspector, darting one of his keen glances at the shrinking cook.

" 'E 'ad a moustache," she quavered at last.

"Large? Or small?"

"In between, like."

But the house-parlourmaid said it was a 'small' moustache.

The Inspector seized on this damning discrepancy. The whole story, it was clear to him, was a tissue of lies, an inept fabrication. They were convicted out of their own mouths – by the contradiction between their own statements.

And their fingerprints were all over the house!

* * *

Dolly Martin came back, in some dudgeon, to Columbine Cottage. Her mood was not improved when she found that her husband had hanged himself, by his braces, in the sitting-room.

* * *

Mrs Cathcart found it difficult to believe that her servants had betrayed her trust in them.

Oh, she accepted the evidence. A lifetime of fearless honesty made it impossible for her long to deceive herself. They had been outside in the rain, and mud had been brought into the house! They had been unable to establish, by any independent witness, at what time they got back to the house! It was a nasty evening – wet and dark – no one had seen them arrive – very convenient! And their fingerprints were to be found in the bedroom and in the dining-room!

"Things look black for them," Mrs Cathcart confided to the Vicar on Friday afternoon. "But they shall have the finest legal brains, in their defence, that I can procure for them."

"Truth will out," said the Vicar hopefully.

"Mr Prynne struck me as a man of keen intelligence."

"Indeed. No question, I fancy, that formidable powers would there be deployed on behalf of the transgressors."

"He so much enjoyed the *blanquettes de veau*."

"As did, dear Mrs Cathcart, all your fortunate guests."

"Yes . . ." Mrs Cathcart remembered, with puzzlement rather than distaste, the curious 'portion' which had given her so much trouble to masticate.

* * *

Mr Prynne gladly accepted the onerous charge placed by Mrs Cathcart on his stalwart shoulders. Never one to slack, not Gordon Prynne! He went so far as to give up his Saturday morning on the 'links' in order to see the criminals, who had been remanded in custody by the Magistrates.

He promised himself, on Sunday evening, a run in his motor out to Mrs Cathcart's to study the 'scene of the crime'.

* * *

"Three pounds," said Millicent, who lay sprawled like some glorious nymph of eld on the hearthrug in front of the fire in Father's den.

"Oh, I say, dash it, that's a bit steep, old thing!" cried Mr Prynne, who had already taken off his trousers.

His shirt-tails did not conceal his excitement.

"Doesn't Millie's friend want a playmate?" asked Millicent cajolingly, lifting the shirt-tail with a mischievous hand. "Yes, he does!"

Reflecting on his fee from Mrs Cathcart, Mr Prynne gave a resigned chuckle, like the 'good sport' he was.

"Right-ho, then!" he conceded.

"Give it to Millie."

"Afterwards," he croaked, pulling, the while, his shirt over his head.

"No, dearest, before. Thanks ever so much. Now do be quick, dear, the others will be freezing in the drawing-room."

He needed no second bidding, not Gordon Prynne! He waxed as ardent as a 'Varsity' man should.

"What a *big* man," said saucy Millicent. "Has little Millie got room for such a big, bad man? Yes, she has!"

"Moy legs gone stiff as buggeree," complained Albert

Monger, emerging from his hiding place behind the Vicar's desk.

Mr Prynne gave a wordless cry. But Millicent had him prisoner! Some of her muscles were very well developed.

"I think, sweetest," said Millicent to Mr Prynne, "that Mrs Cathcart's servants had better plead guilty."

* * *

"The body has been hanging there how long?" queried Doctor Bland on Monday morning.

He was at his most tetchy and forbidding. His young partner Doctor Corbishley had interrupted a roseate reverie of Queenie Perkup in a series of roles for which she was not, perhaps, yet sufficiently physically mature.

"Since noon on Friday, apparently," said Doctor Corbishley. "Mrs Martin said she fainted when she found him, and only came round in time for breakfast today."

"Not the way a lady would have behaved," said Doctor Bland tartly. "But I suppose one can expect no better of the lower middle classes."

Doctor Corbishley flinched.

The sterling young man had become somewhat haggard in appearance. His eyes were haunted by guilt; he started at sudden noises.

Doctor Bland put it down to some ailment about which he did not wish to be told. Edwina Corbishley put it down to bicycling too much. Millicent put it down to his not having three pounds to spend on her. No one else noticed.

"Heigh ho," said Doctor Bland dismissively. "There's

one temporary gentleman the fewer, and small loss, to my way of thinking."

"They'll want me to give evidence at the Inquest," said Doctor Corbishley miserably.

"Which you will do, I am sure, with credit to yourself and to this partnership," said Doctor Bland, waving his colleague away.

He turned his mind inwards again, and with his mind's eye saw Queenie, and with his mind's sensations felt Queenie . . .

* * *

Cook at the Vicarage heard the news almost as soon as anybody.

"It was," she crooned to herself, "for love of me!"

It was a shame, in a way, that Mrs Cathcart's Agnes was in prison. The Major's suicide for love of Cook – that would have been something to talk about over the cocoa and biscuits!

Meanwhile Cook's attitude to life was transformed. She, Florence, had driven a strong man to self-destruction! She was what Agnes called a 'fum fatal'. That meant an adventuress whose mysterious and compelling attraction no man could long resist!

Cook cultivated a new walk, imperious yet seductive. She darted side-long glances at the Vicar, at Doctor Bland, at Vic Mallinson, and at Mr Tomkins.

"They will burn," she told herself, "in the crucible of my love!"

She thought a crucible was part of her anatomy.

* * *

Opinion in the village was sharply divided.

A tiny minority, headed by Tom Melhuish of The Black Swan, held that Major Martin was a good man, an officer and a gentleman, hounded to death by malicious rumours and gossip.

The large majority said that he was an interfering meddler who got no more than he deserved.

All opinion was united in execration of Mrs Martin.

For a day or two this feeling manifested itself only in heads turned ostentatiously away, in refusals to answer greetings, in surly unhelpfulness in the shops.

Then children began to shout after her in the village street.

"Yah!" the pink-cheeked cherubs carolled, "Oo 'ung 'er 'usbing? Oo pinched the money?"

Then the robust lads of the village began throwing stones through her windows at night.

She decided to put Columbine Cottage on the market. But the house-agent in Bogham refused to handle the property.

"With so recent a – hum – tragedy on the premises," said the agent (a great crony of Mr Prynne's at the Golf Club), "I do not think purchasers will be easy to find. I cannot, ha ha ha, see buyers beating a pathway to the door!"

The idea afforded him much mirth. The whole office was in a roar!

"By his braces, wasn't it?" pursued the agent. "No, Mrs Martin, you really must excuse me. Had he shot himself, as gentlemen do, we might have stretched a point. But his braces! Ha ha ha ha ha! I can picture myself explaining *that* to a purchaser!"

* * *

Millicent persuaded Doctor Bland to send her into Bogham in his Daimler.

"Delighted to oblige, little lady," said the Doctor, with a wealth of old-world gallantry. "I expect one day you'll do me a favour, eh?"

"I expect so, Doctor," whispered Millicent, dimpling.

Doctor Bland's chauffeur, who was called Jewkes, wanted Millicent to sit in the front of the car with him. But since he admitted that he had not got three pounds, Millicent pouted and sat by herself, 'like a little Duchess', in the back.

She sold Mrs Cathcart's ruby brooch and her diamond clips and her ear-rings, for £320, to a jeweller called Mr Solomons near the market-place. She had decided to keep the sapphires, since her own eyes were blue! But she knew she was being a silly.

Mr Solomons promised to look at the silver.

Jewkes somehow came by three pounds before it was time to drive homeward. He parked the Daimler on a track in a copse, and joined her, grinning like a monkey, on the capacious leather of the back seat.

She squeezed him tight, and asked him ever so many artless questions.

* * * *

"Here's five pounds," said Millicent to Albert in his

cottage. "It's your share of the money for the jewels, sweetness."

"Ar – for all them sparklers?"

"Yes, dear heart. Now I want you to give me the silver, but not quite all of it. You keep this jug, and this pretty teapot, and these napkin rings. Don't try to sell them, dearest, just keep them safe under the bed."

"Aw roight, Miss," said Albert submissively.

"There's my clever good boy. Are you my clever, good, good, boy?"

"Oo er," said Albert.

"Careful, dear, these ones are pure silk. I'll have three of the five pounds back, sweet, if you're going to be such a big naughty. Thank you, dearest. We'll do Doctor Bland's house next.

CHAPTER THE NINTH

In Which Two Maidens Come To The Dark Tower

"Any news?" asked the Vicar.

"From my – as I suppose I must call him – husband?" replied Mrs Cathcart. "Yes."

"Ah!"

"I have received the courtesy of a brief letter."

"Ah! And what . . .?"

"He has the impertinence to beg, as he puts it, my forgiveness."

"A Christian's duty . . ."

"Certainly, Vicar. I trust I do not need to be reminded of that. I forgive him."

"Saintly woman! I should say, 'Lady'."

"But I will not receive him back into my house. That would be to condone his action, which my conscience would not permit. I have replied to that effect, to what I take to be an accommodation address in London.

"London!" exclaimed the Vicar wonderingly. "The Captain has gone to London? That bodes, I fear, ill."

"As to what it bodes," said Mrs Cathcart magisterially, "I do not pretend to be able to say."

"What news," faltered the Vicar, "from durance vile?"

"The miserable creatures are to plead 'Guilty'. Mr Prynne has persuaded them, with, he confesses to me, the greatest difficulty."

"They were contumacious? Alas!"

"They persisted in an impertinent proclamation of their innocence."

"The trial," said the Vicar, "will, thanks to good Mr Prynne, now be less painful for you."

"But we are no nearer, it seems, to the recovery of my possessions. A Mr Solomons, a most charming and worthy jeweller in Bogham, has undertaken, on our behalf, to keep a 'weather eye out' for any sign or word of my little things."

"Even amongst the Infidel shall be found virtue."

"But as yet to no avail."

"Our prayers go with you in your search."

"And is dear Millicent coming to keep me company again this week?"

"She begs to be allowed to do so."

"Tell her, please, that I have one or two more little silken cast-offs that may please her. Garments that I cannot," Mrs Cathcart tittered, "specify to a male ear."

"Heaven forfend," said the Vicar, horrified, "that I should hear of such things from the lips of a lady! Millicent will be, and I trust show herself, properly grateful."

"I trust so, too," said Mrs Cathcart avidly.

* * *

Millicent made two more visits to Mrs Cathcart. They called them their 'stolen Thursdays', the new servants at Kedleston having adopted the routine of their miserable predecessors.

Millicent was rewarded with several more sets of silk underwear, a sable 'tie', and a small string of pearls that it was supposed the peccant cook and house-parlourmaid had providentially missed.

There was nothing else of Mrs Cathcart's that Millicent wanted.

She refused to come to tea again. For all Mrs Cathcart's blandishments, she said that she was too busy working at her great heavy books, and turning herself into an educated lady.

* * *

Mrs Cathcart took Muriel Figgis aside at the Girls' Sewing Circle. She said she had some cast-off clothes Muriel might like. Muriel said she would visit Mrs Cathcart at tea-time next Thursday afternoon.

* * *

Tom Melhuish of The Black Swan sincerely mourned Major Martin. The Major had never spent less than a pound a week at his local inn, and none of the other regulars came anywhere, in expenditure, near that figure. Tom Melhuish felt genuinely sad when he brooded about his lost turnover; when he got drunk himself he wept into his tankard.

He took to going for walks by himself, after closing time, sobbing at the thought of all the glasses of gin and whisky and beer which he would never again sell to Major Martin.

* * *

Cook at the Vicarage pursued her new career with undiminishing energy but diminishing hope.

It came to her that no one in the village knew she was a 'fum fatal'. She did what she could to show them, but they were used to the idea of her being just the cook at the Vicarage.

If they only knew about the crucible of her love!

One night, when scudding clouds raced across the face of a palely passionate moon, Cook threw a cloak about her body, and sallied forth in search of adventure! Dreamily, buffeted by a wind she scarcely noticed, she allowed her footsteps to take her down the hill – towards The Black Swan!

All there was dark. The drunken singing had stopped. There were no gentlemen about at all.

Abandoning her adventure, Cook turned round and set her face despondently towards home.

She stumbled against something soft, at the roadside – and something clutched at her legs!

She screamed faintly.

"Beg pardon," said Tom Melhuish, thickly, from the ground. "Didn't mean to alarm you. Lost me bearin's, like."

"Ships that pass in the night," said Cook, rapt.

"I 'ates ships," whined Tom Melhuish. "Spent free weeks on a trooper once, sick like a pig, I was, an' all on an empty stummick."

"Mysterious stranger, I am thy lady of darkness!"

"Blackamoor, are you? I 'ad one o' them once. She give me the itches, an' I 'ad to 'ave treatment like I never."

"You shall burn in the crucible of my love!"

"Do what?"

"Fear nothing! Master me!"

She fell to her knees by his side, on the muddy verge of the road, and showered burning kisses on his upturned face.

" 'Ere," he said fretfully, "you stop that. You're makin' me all wet. I'll catch me death, gettin' all wet."

"Oh, how burns my crucible! It's up here."

She guided his limp hand.

"Blimey," he said. "It feels like coconut mattin'. 'Ere, you leave me trousis alone."

"Do not hold back! Let nothing stand in the way of our passion!"

"Well, aw right then, jus' to be friendly," said Tom Melhuish, "but I'm not reelly in the mood."

"Dangles! Oh how sweet!"

" 'Ere, you be careful what you're pullin'. Them things is tender."

"Ravish me!"

"Well, aw right, but I'm not reelly in the mood."

It was a few seconds later that Doctor Bland, driven by Jewkes, returned from a dinner in Bogham. The blazing headlamps blindingly illuminated a scene of startling debauchery! Buttocks of scarcely credible size, mud-smeared, seemed to be bouncing and heaving everywhere. Doctor Bland was entranced, but Jewkes (a family man) was quite shocked.

"That there is Tom Melhuish," Jewkes informed his master.

"And his victim," said Doctor Bland, evincing for the first time some disapproval, "is the cook at the Vicarage."

So, the following morning, Tom Melhuish was arrested for rape, and remanded in custody by the Bogham Magistrates.

* * *

Doctor Corbishly called at the Vicarage to examine Cook. Doctor Bland had refused to do so.

"My patients in that house," said Doctor Bland sharply to his partner, "are above stairs. You may visit whom you please."

Cook's idea of an examination went far beyond Doctor Corbishley's idea of an examination. As she was twice his weight, and possessed four or five times his strength, her ideas prevailed.

Doctor Corbishley returned to the Surgery.

"Is she a virgin?" asked Doctor Bland, with a flicker of interest.

"No," said Doctor Corbishley, in a small, exhausted voice.

"Then clearly Melhuish raped her. You will say so in court."

* * *

Doctor Bland called at the Vicarage, too, to make sure (he said) that all was well with his patients there. The Vicar was out, on a pastoral visit. Millicent received the affable physician.

"The lower classes have no resilience," said Doctor Bland, with refined distaste. "That woman might easily go all to pieces, while a lady would simply laugh the whole thing off. So I just looked in, my dear, to make sure *you* were all right."

"Oo yes, thank you ever so much," said Millicent in her shy little voice. "Thanks ever so much for asking."

They chatted for a little while. Millicent confided that it was her life's ambition to do good, and to leave the world a better place than she found it.

Doctor Bland said that there was a particular piece of good which she could do at once, if she was serious about doing good.

Millicent exclaimed that of course she was serious about doing good! She would do anything, anything, that would make the world a better place.

Doctor Bland asked if Millicent knew the Perkup children.

Millicent admitted, with a tiny shudder, that she knew the Perkup children.

Doctor Bland said that he was a *little* worried about Queenie Perkup, the eldest. He thought it his duty to examine her.

"Examine her?" echoed Millicent, wide-eyed.

"Her tonsils," explained Doctor Bland quickly. "Her adenoids."

"How terribly, terribly kind of you, Doctor Bland, to concern yourself with that poor, poor child."

Doctor Bland said that, by a curious coincidence, he, too, wanted to make the world a better place.

Millicent agreed to bring Queenie Perkup to Doctor Bland's house on Wednesday, early in the evening.

* * *

"Wednesday, dearest," said Millicent to Albert Monger. "All the servants will be out."

"Ar."

"That nice Mr Jewkes told me the servants always have Wednesday afternoon off. I expect that's why Doctor Bland wants to see Queenie then."

"What 'e goin' fer tew dew wi' Queenie?"

"Look at her adenoids."

* * *

Dolly Martin got a letter from Dads. He said he was that shocked and horrified about poor Ernest, whom he had always liked and admired, and thought Dolly was lucky to get. He said he was not one to lay blame, but *he*, Dads, never felt like doing himself in, and *he* had a good, faithful, hard-working wife, so if Ernest had felt like doing himself in, it followed that Dolly had *not* been a good, faithful, hard-working wife.

So what with one thing and another, and times not being easy, Dads was stopping Dolly's allowance.

* * *

Millicent instantly recognised a potential rival. The evil in Queenie Perkup's face was unmistakable, even through its layers of grime. There was character there, too, thought Millicent – cunning, a sharp animal intelligence of which poor sweet Albert had hardly a glimmer.

She may be useful, thought Millicent. Or she may be jolly inconvenient one day!

The younger children, Mabel and little Phyllis, wanted to come to Doctor Bland's house, too. Queenie screamed at them, using a few words which Millicent had learned from

Albert, and others which she had never heard. They cowered back into the disgusting little cottage of their squalid and crapulous grandmother.

Millicent led Queenie the half mile to Doctor Bland's house. She glanced round once, and confirmed that Albert, shambling and corrupt, was faithfully following a hundred yards behind them.

Doctor Bland's house was approached by a carriage-drive, the only real carriage-drive in the immediate neighbourhood, the only one up which carriages could be imagined rolling, behind their spanking 'pairs' or 'fours'. Trees parted to reveal a big sweep of gravel, beyond which rose the purple late Victorian brick of The Towers.

It was a very large house for a country doctor. Doctor Bland was a very rich man for a country doctor. He had been the beneficiary of a number of wills, throughout his career, of elderly female patients. Some of these wills had been contested by the families of the departed ladies, on grounds of 'undue influence' and the like. All the cases had been settled out of court. The lawyers did well, and Doctor Bland did well too. One of the largest of the legacies was that of his wife, who had been a good many years older than himself. She had died of a mysterious illness in 1903, some of whose symptoms were amusingly similar to those of mercury poisoning.

The sky was almost dark when Millicent led Queenie towards the imposing edifice. Queenie whimpered and struggled, but Millicent held fast to her hand. She wanted Doctor Bland thoroughly preoccupied while Albert burgled the house.

They crunched across the huge sweep of gravel. A few

windows glowed richly behind heavy damask curtains. They climbed great granite steps to the front door. Queenie screamed a few unintelligible words of terrified blasphemy, but Millicent held tight to her skinny little arm.

Millicent heard, in a moment of silence, the crunch of a stolen and ill-fitting boot on the gravel behind. Albert was there, lurking in the near darkness, waiting for her signal.

Millicent pulled a heavy, black metal ring at the end of a chain. A bell clanged far away.

Instantly, as though he had been waiting (avid) just inside, Doctor Bland himself opened the prodigious front door! Of course, there was no one else in the house to do so. They had the place all to themselves!

Doctor Bland was tall, cadaverous, vulturine. He was dressed in a formal style, somewhat old fashioned, with high wing collar and pearl-grey spats. Jewels winked from his cuffs and tie pin.

Millicent wondered if, in examining Queenie's adenoids, Doctor Bland would take off his shirt and tie.

"Ah, my dears," cried Doctor Bland in his bluff countryman's way (more 'Squire', he, than professional man), "welcome, welcome indeed."

Throwing the door wide for them, he sketched a mock-solemn bow.

Millicent dragged Queenie across the threshold and into the cavernous hall.

Doctor Bland shut the front door behind them, locked it with a key as large as a golf club, and shot, with a flourish, a bolt the size of a gun barrel.

There were to be no interruptions at The Towers.

Queenie snarled and gibbered, like a trapped animal.

Indoors, she gave off an acrid, indescribable smell of jungle or sewer. Fastidious Millicent wrinkled her pert nose in distaste.

Albert, she was thinking, would have to come in by a window.

Far away across the hall, a grandfather clock struck five. The sudden 'bong' that commenced its melodious chime was quite startling! Queenie screamed – pulled away from Millicent – and sped away like a terrified spider up the stairs!

"Drat," said Doctor Bland.

His face darkened with anger. He emitted a barbaric hunting cry, and, showing remarkable energy for a man of his advanced years, bolted up the stairs after Queenie.

Millicent strolled into the opulent drawing-room to open a window for Albert.

CHAPTER THE TENTH

In Which The Hunt Goes From View To Death

Like a naughty rabbit, like a vexatious mouse, Queenie Perkup sped along the great dark caverns of the upstairs passages of The Towers. She had the advantage of youth, but Doctor Bland that of 'local knowledge'. He thundered after her, still shouting incoherently, his face almost black with rage. He was not accustomed to being thwarted, the haughty lord of The Towers, by a grimy, reeking, undernourished peasant waif!

If terror lent Queenie wings, be sure that rage and desire lent them to our thundering and bellowing doctor!

The inevitable at last happened. Queenie found herself in a passage which ended in a blank wall!

"Ha ha!" cried Doctor Bland, insensate. "Tally Ho!"

Queenie slipped into a room, a great, gaunt, black bedroom with a yawning fireplace. The Doctor followed her. The room had but one door! She was trapped. He switched on the electrics. The chamber was flooded with harsh light from a great brass electrolier hanging on a chain from the ceiling.

Doctor Bland shut the door. He locked it, and pocketed

the key. He grinned wolfishly, panting from exertion and excitement.

What now? She is so young, so thin. What are his intentions? Is it possible? Will there be room?

Queenie screamed and gibbered, in what might have been demotic Portuguese, or a little known dialect of darkest Africa. He roared back, no more intelligible than she, a mixture of reproof and endearment.

Never had a slip of girlie so taken the Doctor's fancy!

He groped towards her, grinning now like a hyena, thin lips drawn back from long yellow teeth, huge white hands, claw-like, the fingernails extremely clean, black-haired along the backs of the fingers, poised to clutch – and then – what?

She shrank away, chattering like a furious monkey.

He grabbed! She twisted away, and darted beyond the bed. And so began the maddest game of 'tag' or 'catch-as-catch-can' ever played, I trow, in that sombre chamber! He roaring, she screaming, he lunging forward, she dancing backward, he circling this way, she darting that way, he shedding (for mobility) his coat, waistcoat, tie and stiff wing collar, her rags catching on this and tearing on that – never was amorous suitor more tormented, never bashful nymph more evasive!

They seemed likely to go on all night.

* * *

Millicent knew her way about, for was she not of that august and select body, the 'visiting list' of The Towers? And had she not heard the mansion's owner expatiating anent the value of his collection of antique snuff boxes (left to him by an infatuated patient), of his silver (the property, once, of his late wife's family), and of his great gloomy paintings?

Millicent had decided not to steal the paintings, this time.

Albert, she noticed with approval, had again omitted to wear gloves. Probably he owned no gloves, and had been too inept or forgetful to steal any. She herself had put her little kid gloves onto her little pink fingers, the moment she was inside the house.

From far away, from a great height and a great distance, came the roars and shrieks of the Prince and his Beggarmaid.

"He is still looking at her adenoids," remarked Millicent to Albert. "Perhaps it tickles."

"Ar," said Albert, uncertain what, or where, Queenie's adenoids might be, but ashamed to display his ignorance. Sometimes Millicent made him feel quite inferior, even unworthy.

On his dainty Captain's instructions, Albert levered open the door of the glass fronted cabinet in which, on velvet shelves, reposed the collection of snuff boxes. There was a good deal of splintering when he forced open the door, and one of the panes of glass broke.

All this made a considerable noise. Albert turned to Millicent, his mouth open and drooling in sudden panic.

She cocked to one side her neat little coppery head (for all the world like a birdie in Nature's garden), listening to the animal noises from upstairs. They continued uninterrupted.

"No need to fuss, old thing," she murmured soothingly, matching to these comforting words her usual comforting gesture.

After a farewell squeeze, she began to transfer, with

careful gloved fingers, the treasures in the cabinet to the sack Albert had brought.

Then they went into the Butler's Pantry for the silver.

* * *

Shirt tails flapping, nether garments somewhat indecorously disarranged, Doctor Bland lunged once again at his tantalising quarry – and once again she darted out of his reach, her scream like that of a small demented rodent.

The love-struck fellow's face was now purple – dangerously suffused, a well-wisher might have thought, with blood – and he foamed and dribbled from a wide and gasping mouth.

It was, perhaps, more regrettable than surprising that he should suddenly clutch his chest, stagger, fall to his knees, and then collapse at full length upon the floor, victim of a fatal heart attack.

Queenie approached the body cautiously, chirruping to herself words which, if interpreted, would not have seemed, to a person of strict behaviour, suitable in the presence of death.

Satisfied that he would no longer chase her, she examined the garments which he had discarded here and there on the floor. She found the pearl pin in his tie, the coins in his waistcoat pocket, and the notes in the leather folder in the inside pocket of his jacket. She had never touched one of these last before, but she had seen them in the hands of others, and suspected them of usefulness. She stuck the tie pin in the tattered and disgusting singlet which, only by the greatest exercise of charity, could have been called a blouse.

She thrust the banknotes under the perished elastic of her discoloured knickers. The coins she clutched.

She opened the window, and climbed without difficulty to the ground by way of a sturdy creeper.

* * *

"They seem to have stopped singing," said Millicent, head adorably on one side in a listening pose. "I wonder why?"

" 'E cotched un," suggested Albert.

"Do you think so, dear heart? And so do I! Will he come downstairs, I wonder?"

"Ow, Miss!" wailed Albert, giving, by the collapse of his degenerate chin, evidence of renewed panic.

"So," said masterful Millie, "we'll nip out of the window you came in by."

They hurried to the drawing-room. Glancing at the burgled cabinet, Millicent was pleased to see that Albert's greasy and malformed fingers had left copious, unmistakable fingerprints all over the glass. As he opened the window, under her brisk direction, he left many more fingerprints there.

"Give Millie a hand, sweetest, she carolled cajolingly, climbing onto the windowsill.

Perched half in, half out, she looked for all the world like a saucy kiddie at play on a hobby-horse!

Albert, listening with painful anxiety for sounds of descent from above, handed out the laden sack to his Millicent. He followed her out onto the rose-bed, which there nuzzled the lofty wall of The Towers. He entirely obscured her footprints, with his own, in the soft earth of the bed.

"Still no sound," murmured Millicent, adorably pensive. "I expect he's operating."

* * *

The parlourmaid at The Towers, returning to duty, noticed that a window was open, from the billowing of the curtains in the brisk November breeze.

She shut the window, frowning, instantly inclined to suspect the kitchenmaid, who was up to any mischief, and did not know her place, and had no business to be so much as setting foot in the Master's drawing-room.

She did not notice the damage to the cabinet, owing to her mood of vexation with the kitchenmaid. No one else in the household noticed it either, nor the damage in the butler's pantry.

The servants settled down to their 'meat tea', surprised, but rather pleased than the reverse, that the Doctor should be out.

* * *

Queenie Perkup scampered home to her grandmother's cottage. She made a stealthy entry, not relishing – not she! – the leathering which that dame had been known to administer to errant scamps.

But her grandmother had stolen enough money to get drunk, and thus posed no problem.

Queenie's little sisters bombarded her with eager questions, which, by some miracle of intuition, she understood. She screamed them into tearful silence, jabbing Mabel additionally, with the tie pin. Then she put her little 'earnings' in a tin box, and hid the box under a fallen apple tree in the dark garden, 'against a rainy day'.

* * *

Millicent let Albert keep two large, distinctive pieces of Sheffield plate – five-branched candlesticks, which had graced Doctor Bland's mahogany when he gave one of his famous dinner parties. She took the rest of the silver, and the snuff boxes.

* * *

Doctor Corbishley was obliged, that evening, to visit once again the Vicarage cook, and submit his frail little body to her bone-cracking embraces.

His few experiences with Millicent had not at all prepared him for anyone like the Vicarage cook. She was too big – far too big – everything about her was too big. Her teeth were too big: also the gaps between her teeth. Her legs were too big: also the gap between her legs.

Doctor Corbishley had once, as a child, with his sister Edwina, been taken on holiday to Scotland. Walking over the springy heather on some high hillside, he had stumbled into a mud-hole, invisible under the rank vegetation which surrounded it, treacherous in the last degree. The mud hole was perhaps a foot across, but of bottomless depth. It was black and reeking, giving off noxious gas: its horrible and decaying smell lingered for hours. It was wet, and slimy. It was endowed with a mysterious suction which swallowed, engulfed, pulled inwards and downwards. The mud hole had given Doctor Corbishley nightmares; the thought of it made him shudder with terror and distaste. He hoped never again to encounter such a thing. But now he had, between the mighty legs of the Vicarage cook.

He was much too frightened of her to reject her ardent advances, or to put up more than the briefest and most token resistance. It was not his fault. None of it was his fault. But the phrase 'gross professional misconduct' rang through his head like a gong.

* * *

Mrs Cathcart was greatly shocked at the news of Doctor Bland's disappearance. It even occurred to her to put off Muriel Figgis' promised visit, 'until a more fitting time'. But this idea was no sooner examined than discarded. Poor Doctor Bland, wherever he might be, would not benefit by Mrs Cathcart having a lonely afternoon.

Muriel accordingly came, after school, her little pig eyes flickering with a mixture of nervousness and greed.

"Do you like this dress, dear? It is almost new, you know. You would be amazed if I told you how much it cost. More than people like your father earn, I daresay, in a whole year. Shall Muriel try it on? But not over this one, dear. This one must come off, mustn't it? Hold still, dearest, while Mrs Cathcart wrestles with all these naughty, stubborn buttons . . ."

* * *

The judge summed up at the trial, which had been greatly

expedited by their plea of 'Guilty', of Mrs Cathcart's cook and house-parlourmaid.

"The only point in mitigation that can be found, even by your own legal advisers, in this most shocking and deplorable case, is that you have pleaded 'Guilty'. That has saved the time of the Court. It has saved my time, that of learned counsel, that of the twelve good men and true who are empanelled in the jury-box.

"It would be a greater point in mitigation if I were able to detect any signs that you were genuinely repentant for the crime – I will rather say, for the *sin* – which you have committed, and if you were to have assisted the police in the recovery of the property that you cynically and ungratefully stole.

"I repeat, ungratefully. This is, perhaps, of the many despicable aspects of your crime, the one which will most outrage all decent people. An employer of the greatest generosity showed you both the most signal and continual kindness. How did you reward her? She placed her trust in you. How did you repay that trust? She had, herself, recently suffered a grievous personal tragedy, in the loss of an esteemed mate. How did you comfort her, in that hour when she was, if ever woman was, entitled to your loyalty, to your especial consideration and regard?

"I will tell you how you rewarded her kindness. I will tell you how you repaid her trust. I will tell you how you comforted her in her hour of bitter grief. You stole from her all that she had of value, the precious mementoes of departed kinsfolk, which she daily viewed in her own house with an affection and regard far beyond mere appreciation of monetary value.

"But that monetary value is not to be regarded as insignificant. By no means. Far from it. Were the objects you stole, and about the present whereabouts of which you continue to be obdurately silent, worth some few pence only, or even shillings, I could find it possible to contemplate the exercise of considerable leniency, in view especially of your apparently blameless records. I say 'apparently' advisedly, because no right-thinking person could find it easy to believe that your cold-hearted treachery was not the culmination of lives of depravity and undetected crime in the past.

"But the objects you stole were worth not a few pence, nor a few shillings, nor yet a few pounds, but hundreds of pounds. Perhaps thousands of pounds.

"You will each go to prison for twenty years. Take them away."

* * *

The routine of Doctor Bland's household became somewhat irregular, even sloppy, owing to the continued absence of the Master's eagle eye.

One consequence (and not the least delightful) was that the housemaid was able to contemplate entertaining the under-gardener in the demure comfort of a bedroom, rather than submitting to his 'experiments' in the potting-shed.

The chamber she selected for her first 'party' had the virtue of remoteness. It was an unused room in a little used part of the house, where the parlourmaid was unlikely to come snooping at a person and her boy.

That she found the door locked surprised but did not dismay her. She had duplicate keys for all the bedrooms.

This was an arrangement made long before, with another housemaid, when Doctor Bland suspected his wife, then still alive, of 'funny business' with her Cocker spaniel.

Screams from the housemaid, when she went into the room, brought the parlourmaid. Screams from the parlourmaid brought the cook and kitchenmaid. Screams from all four of them brought Jewkes the chauffeur from his 'berth' over the coach-house.

"The pore Master passed beyond, Mister Jewkes, in the middle of undressin'," explained the parlourmaid to the chauffeur. "It give me ever such a turn to see 'im without 'is trousis."

"Why was 'e undressin' in 'ere?" musingly enquired the housemaid, thwarted (poor nymph) of her own fun.

"There's mysteries 'ere," pronounced Jewkes at last. "Dark secricks. I'll get the car out an' fetch that Doctor Corbishley."

Doctor Corbishley, when fetched, was a good deal flustered. He had never, of course, attended his awesome senior partner in a professional capacity, Doctor Bland naturally preferring to consult an expensive practitioner in Bogham, or a still more expensive one in London. Doctor Corbishley wished one or both of these giants were here now. He was abashed at the thought of touching Doctor Bland, dead though the latter was reported to be.

He could not overcome a feeling of impertinence, even of impropriety, when he knelt by his revered confrère: especially as Doctor Bland's bare legs were in colour, though not in texture or size, unnervingly reminiscent of those of the Vicarage cook.

*   *   *

"Oo Mr Solomons," said Millicent, looking as stern as her roguish little face allowed. "You didn't give me half enough! The judge said those jewels were worth ever so many thousand pounds! You must be a bit more decent next time, or I'll go to the police and tell them you bought the things."

"Then you'll be off to prison yourself, Miss," said Mr Solomons. But his nervous eye belied the bluff confidence of his manner.

"Of course I won't," cried Millicent. "Don't be such a juggins. I'm only an innocent little country girl, a Vicar's daughter. I think the judge and the jury would believe me, don't you? I think they'd be awfully cross with you if you tried to drag me into it. I should think the judge would send you to prison for twice as long."

"I need a little time," babbled Mr Solomons. "I need a buyer. I need to raise the ready cash."

Three days later Millicent got £700 for Mrs Cathcart's silver and some of Doctor Bland's.

She gave Albert eight pounds. He immediately gave her back three of them, in return for ten minutes on his mother's bed in the cottage.

"The next place," remarked Millicent thoughtfully, "had better be Mr Solomon's shop. What's the matter, sweetness? Don't you love Millie today? Oh. Well, you can't have the three pounds back."

CHAPTER THE ELEVENTH

In Which A Jeweller Meets His Match

The circumstances of Doctor Bland's death were a topic of intense speculation in the village. From parlourmaid, housemaid, kitchenmaid, cook, chauffeur and gardeners came varying accounts and theories, the latter being elaborated to a point approaching fantasy, during discussion among such leaders of local thought as Mr Figgis and Mrs Mallinson.

Why had the poor gentleman taken down his trousers in an unused spare bedroom in an unused part of the house?

" 'E wanted to 'ave a rub," opined Bobby Tomkins, himself so devoted to this new diversion that he could not imagine a man not spending every spare moment at it.

This theory gained wide and immediate acceptance among Bobby's contemporaries. Not a few of the grown-ups were disposed to accept it likewise.

The servants at the mansion continued to take things easy after the body of their master had been removed, with the result that it was a few more days before the disappearance of the snuff-boxes and silver was discovered. Suspicion was focussed on the servants, but to the intense disappointment of the Inspector in Bogham, they were all able to account for their movements. Evidence of an outside job was also conclusive – the open window remembered by the parlourmaid, the footprints in the flower-bed below it, observed by the under-gardener, the fingerprints which matched those neither of servants nor of the deceased.

It was difficult to hypothesise a link between burglary and death. Why (reasoned some of the best brains in the local force) would a gentleman drop his trousers upstairs, because there was a burglar downstairs?

The servants were given notice, and the house was to be put up for sale by the executors.

* * *

"Let's pick primroses," said Muriel Figgis, as she bicycled home after school with Bobby Tomkins.

Primroses? In November? The idea was absurd. Yet mark with what eager zest young Bobby leaps from his wheel and follows the damsel into the shady tangles of Craddock's Wood!

"I'm seein' *'er* again Thursday," said Muriel, reminded of her new patroness by the touch of Bobby's fingers as he undid her.

"What 'zackly do she do, then?" asked Bobby.

"Jus' prods, mos'ly."

"Like this?"

"Sorta. An' down 'ere."

"Coo," breathed Bobby. "Kin I try that?"

"If you like. On'y that bit's more for strokin'."

"Coo. You mean like a dog?"

"Sorta."

Bobby's hand, a-tremble, explored new and delightful mysteries!

"Fancy," he said at last, in wonderment, " 'avin' a 'ole, 'stead o' stickin' out."

"What's so funny about 'avin' a 'ole?" asked Muriel crisply, leaping (woman like) to the defence of her sex.

"It's easier goin' wee-wee with what I got," explained Bobby.

"You think *that's* what it's for?"

"It's convenient, like. You kin point it where it's goin', like."

"It's not just for goin' wee-wee," she informed him, loftily.

"Course not! Oo said it was? It's for rubbin'."

"It's for goin' in 'ere," she said. "Where yore finger gorn in."

But Bobby found this too incredible.

* * *

Jewkes, under threat of dismissal, was heavy-hearted. The 'berth' was a good one, the 'pickings' considerable. Petty theft had enabled him to visit the Vicarage young lady twice since the first beautiful occasion in the back of the Daimler. Now the future was obscure, and the wife unfairly blaming him for it. Jewkes felt hard done by.

He was running a leather over the Daimler in the coach-house (the car, too, was to be sold) when to his surprise the Vicarage young lady appeared.

"I saw Mrs Jewkes going off into the village," she said, "so we can have a nice private talk."

"Talk, Miss?"

"I know what you'd rather do, you naughty boy, and so would I, if you've got the money, but honestly and truly we must have a little talk. You've got to drive me and a friend to Bogham tonight, late at night, and after a time you must bring us back."

"Oh no, Miss," said Jewkes instantly, "anything to oblige, Miss, but that's out of the question. Oh no. I couldn't possibly, not if it was ever so."

"Oh, fiddlesticks!" cried Millicent, catching that 'bee-stung' lower lip in those little pearly teeth that could do such astonishing things to a man's funny-bits.

Even hurt a bit, once or twice, thought Jewkes, shaken by concupiscent memories.

"Oh Miss!" the great baby blurted out, "I does wish I 'ad three quid!"

"I'll let you off the three pounds, dear, if you'll ever so kindly drive us to Bogham as I said."

"Oh no, Miss . . . Even if . . . No, it's out of the question!"

Millicent put her own rosy finger-tip to her lips. First she kissed it, her eyes dreamy. Then she gently bit it, many times, very fast, with those little sharp teeth, those pearly pointed weapons of pain and pleasure . . .

Jewkes, hardly able to bring the words out, said that he would drive Miss and her friend to Bogham.

* * *

When Jewkes found that Albert Monger was to be his other passenger, he demurred. His objection was, in part, to the smell which, inevitably, Albert would leave on the

Daimler's impeccable upholstery; it was, in part, to having a witness to the nibbling of his funny-bits by Millicent, to which he looked forward with feverish anxiety.

"Albert won't look, will you, dear?" Millicent said comfortingly.

According to her amiable habit, she accompanied the words with a gesture, or caress, like that with which she had so often brought courage, or resignation, to Albert. Jewkes found it surprising in a well brought up young lady.

Albert, behind Jewkes' back, meanwhile winked at Millicent, the effect repulsive in the last degree, the doglike and misshapen features being further pulled into a nightmare of hideous distortion. He licked his yellow lips with a yellow tongue, while a dribble of saliva, of a darker and more opaque yellow, rolled down his spotted and receding chin.

Millicent (the tomboy) winked back.

And so the party started merrily off – Albert in the back, Millicent beside the chauffeur in the front.

It was at once clear that Jewkes' objections to the way Albert would make the car smell were abundantly justified. In a confined space he was almost overwhelming, like a piece of ancient and pullulating green cheese.

Millicent silenced Jewkes' objections by undoing his trouser-buttons as he drove.

They saw no one on the roads or in the town. Jewkes parked the car in a side-street near the market place. He promised to wait. Millicent said they would not keep him long. She gave him a final nip with her fingernails (pain almost unendurable, pleasure beyond imagining!) and scrambled out of the chariot.

Albert, after some trouble with the door-handle, shambled after her, carrying a suitcase stolen from a commercial traveller who was staying at The Black Swan. (Mrs Melhuish welcomed gentlemen residents while her husband was in prison awaiting trial.)

Millicent's plan was simple – indeed, well tried.

Mr Solomons lived over his shop. If he was out, there was no problem. If he was in, Millicent would keep him busy upstairs, while Albert filled the suitcase downstairs.

Millicent was again wearing gloves, Albert not.

It was very dark in the little street where Mr Solomon's shop was. But light came from a window above the shop.

He was there.

Millicent pulled at a bell. It jangled in the darkness behind the heavy door.

She pulled again and again. She kept the bell a-jangle until it must have awakened the veriest sleepy-head!

At last the small window above opened. A sleek, balding head appeared against the light.

"Yoo-hoo," warbled Millicent softly. "It's Millie."

"My God," said Mr Solomons, "what are you doing here at this time of night?"

"Nothing special. Millie's ever so bored and lonely, and as you're much the bestest friend she's got in Bogham, I wondered if you'd like to amuse me for a few minutes."

"That I will," vouchsafed the worthy jeweller. "Wait right there, girlie."

To Albert, in the shadows, Millicent whispered a command. He replied with one of the moist grunts which, in the main, did service with him for speech. Even in the open air he smelled like a very dangerous piece of cheese.

Millicent quite liked the smell – it reminded her of so many happy times – but she wondered of she were not growing a little bored with it.

From inside the shop came the sounds of bolts, chain, and lock. The door opened to reveal Mr Solomons in woolly cardigan and carpet-slippers, smoking a cigarette in a holder, grinning rather wetly, and blinking with unconcealed excitement through gold-rimmed spectacles.

"Well, well, well," he chortled, "this is a lovely surprise and no mistake."

"I can only stay for a few minutes."

"You're welcome for as long as you like. You can stay all night, if you like."

"Gosh, that would be scrumptious, but I must get home to Father."

This (alas) was nothing but a tarradiddle! The Vicar was away! He was not expected home until tea-time the following day. Cook and Millicent had the Vicarage to themselves, except that Doctor Corbishley had said he would look in to see Cook some time during the evening.

Millicent followed Mr Solomons into the shop. He locked the door behind her, leaving the key in the lock.

"As you're not staying long," he remarked, "I'll trust to the lock, and do the bolts when you leave."

Naughty Millicent did so much admire the great shiny metal bolts, the heavy chain of the door! And while she was admiring them, she slipped the key out of the lock, and popped it down the front of her frock!

Brr! It was cold against her soft pink skin.

They went through a door at the back of the shop, into a kind of workroom. Stairs led upstairs to a landing. Off the landing was a room let, ever so snug, where Mr Solomons lived.

Millicent flew about the room like a little bird, or moth. She gave cries of pleasure at all she saw. To hear her, you would have thought the simple chamber was the very boudoir of a royal infanta!

"And a ducky little window," she warbled. "Does it open?"

" 'Course it opens," said Mr Solomons, surveying with a mixture of indulgence and impatience the cavortings of his young friend.

"I don't believe it does, so there!" cried saucy Millicent, casting over her shoulder a coquettish glance.

Yet well she knew (the minx) that the window truly opened – as Mr Solomons himself had opened it, when she rang and rang his bell!

She opened the little casement, plunging her hand, the while, down the front of her frock.

She held the key!

She dropped it out of the window, giving a little shriek to hide the noise of its fall in the street below.

"What's biting you, girlie," asked Mr Solomons. "And why did you put your hand where I'd like to put mine?"

"Millie's got ever such a horrid old itch down here," said Millicent, giving one of her adorable pouts. "And it's such an awkward place to scratch!"

"I don't mind helping," riposted he.

"Oo, will you? That would be scrumptious! I'll sit down here, shall I, so you can reach down better."

Down the front of the dainty frock went the rogue's hand! To scratch? Not it! The fingers found better things to do.

"That's lovely, dear," said Millicent, listening for Albert below.

Mr Solomons brought his other hand into play, Millicent, too, became busy with her fingers, even taking off her gloves, the better to do those mischievous things that seemed to give her friends so much innocent enjoyment.

There was a crash from below! It was an awesome noise – as though a bomb had exploded!

"My God, what's that," cried Mr Solomons, withdrawing at once his moist and trembling hands.

"Mice, dear," said Millicent soothingly.

He struggled to get away – but she held him fast! A dingle-dangle in each hand (stronger little hands than they looked, with ten sharp nails!) she would not let her admirer leave her!

"Leggo!" cried Mr Solomons. "Ouch!"

"Millie's got a prisoner," gurgled Millicent, "Two prisoners."

He implored. He beseeched. She laughed!

He seized her wrists. She tightened her grip. He shrieked!

There was another crash from below, yet louder than the first!

A frown marred for a moment the perfect marble of our heroine's brow. She thought what a clumsy duffer her Albert was.

Her prisoner shrieked again, perhaps at the thought of the destruction in the shop below – perhaps at the cruel grip of Millicent's hands.

He struck her!

O coward and bully, O ungentlemanly cad! He smote our Millie full in the face with his hand! Thus does greed turn men into the veriest brutes.

She gave a little cry – more (I trow) of astonishment than of pain – and let the dingle-dangles go!

Off down the stairs like a rabbit ran Mr Solomons, buttoning his trousers as he went.

"Oh fiddlesticks," pouted Millicent to herself, ever so vexed at this turn of events.

She tidied her own fashionable costume, somewhat disarranged, and put on her gloves. She went downstairs more sedately than her host, arriving at ground level in time to see Albert crack Mr Solomon's skull with a brass carriage lamp.

"What a clumsy you are," she reproved him.

Albert drooled with horror at what he had done. Terror increased the stench he gave off.

"Have you packed everything I told you into the case, dear?" asked Millicent.

"Ar."

"Good boy. And where is the key?"

"Oi left un in door."

"Oh, goodie. Wait here just a tick, then, sweetie."

Millicent picked up the suitcase, which was mighty heavy for a little thing like her, and tripped out of the shop. Albert waited inside, as he had been bidden.

Millicent shut the door, and locked it from outside. She dropped the key down a grating in the road: then she went off to find Mr Jewkes and the Daimler.

On the way home, Mr Jewkes warmly agreed with his fair passenger that neither of them would say anything about their spin in the Daimler. Mr Jewkes would be in trouble if anyone found out he had been using the car 'on the sly'.

They stopped the car in a wood for a few minutes on the way.

When Millicent got back to the Vicarage, she hid the suitcase in some bushes at the bottom of the garden. Then she went to bed. It had been quite an exhausting day!

CHAPTER THE TWELFTH

In Which Adam Encounters Two Eves

"He said what?" cried Millicent, eyes wide with dismay.

The Inspector spread his great red hands in a deprecating gesture.

"I'm that sorry to trouble you with 'is nonsense, Miss," he said.

"Oh, don't, don't apologise," cried Millicent. "It is your duty to ask me about it! We must all do our duty, all the time!"

"Thank you, Miss," said the Inspector gratefully, put quite at his ease by his dainty hostess. "The man Alfred Monger was hevidently surprised in a burglarious hact by the shopkeeper, and killed 'im with a blow on the 'ead with a 'eavy hinstrument, to wit, a lamp, brass, carriage."

"Poor, poor man! Did he – tell me that he did not – have a wife and little, little children?"

"No, Miss. Don't weep no tears for the victim – 'e was a scoundrill 'isself."

"Then," said Millicent, her great eyes misting softly, "he needs our prayers all the more."

"Neighbours 'earin' a ruckuss or disturbance," continued the Inspector, 'made contact with the Hofficer on the beat, 'oo forced a hentry, and found the man Monger a-slobberin' over the corpse of 'is victim."

"Slobbering, Inspector?"

"Or a-blubberin', Miss. The Hofficer used both terms in his report."

"It is a dreadful, dreadful story," sighed Millicent. "I am only a little, ignorant school-girlie, and it comes as a horrid shock to me to hear about such things."

"Duty or no, Miss, I'm that sorry to defile your delicate hears with haccounts of 'orrible crimes of violence."

"Forgive me for being such a silly-billy," said Millicent, looking at the bluff Inspector with piteous appeal, "but why have you come all this way to tell me about it?"

"The man Monger 'as made the hallegation, Miss, that you was 'is haccomplice."

Millicent gave a cry of horror and astonishment. She was ever so upset! She seemed likely to faint.

The Inspector patted her hand. Soon afterwards he took leave of her dainty self, and of that Godly man her reverend father, and went to see how his lads were getting on searching the Mongers' cottage.

They had found some pieces of silver stolen from Mrs Cathcart, and two large Sheffield plate candlesticks stolen from the residence of the late Doctor Bland.

Albert Monger was remanded in custody on charges of murder, robbery with violence, breaking and entering, and receiving stolen goods. Other charges were expected to follow, when the police had concluded their investigations.

* * *

"I opine," said the Police Surgeon, "that simple contiguity

is the explanation for the aberration from which this creature suffers. He is quite subnormal, you know, almost an idiot. I imagine the Defence will plead diminished responsibility. I picture the man Monger glimpsing little Miss Willis – what an enchanting child, by the bye, the very type or pattern of innocent girlhood such as we all too rarely see in these degenerate days – I picture Monger, I say, glimpsing Miss Millicent as she goes about in the quaint, old-world garden of the Vicarage, and from these furtive glimpses weaving a tapestry of fantasy, as infants and idiots do, and at last almost convincing himself that she was indeed his companion in these dark deeds. Heigh ho, who shall explore the dark recesses of a criminal lunatic's mind?"

The Inspector's eyes glazed, and his mouth fell a little open, as he tried to digest the Police Surgeon's theory.

"You mean, 'e's barmy?" he said at last.

"I greatly fear so."

"Then 'e'll dodge the noose. What a bleedin' shame."

* * *

Doctor Corbishley was in a state approaching complete disintegration, mental and physical. His body, always skinny, had become emaciated. His expression, always nervous, had become haunted. His voice, always diffident, had become a terrified and exhausted whisper.

He had neither the spirit nor the cash for any more of those once-prized quarter-hours with Millicent – especially now that she had raised her charges to a daunting five sovereigns!

And the Vicarage cook was rapidly destroying what little remained of his manhood and sanity.

She was so big! Her demands were so insatiable and so frequent! He was so frightened of her!

Edwina was appalled at the change in him. She longed for a confidante – a real pal such as she had known in Croydon – but here there was no one she could talk to. She thought Mrs Cathcart and Millicent Willis too stuck up for her. The village women thought *she* was too stuck up for *them*. She fell between the local aristocracy and the common people, utterly isolated. She had many a private cry about it. She was dreadfully lonely, and beside herself with worry about her baby brother.

She even wondered if he was in love, a condition about which she had read. She hoped not. She found the whole subject nasty.

* * *

"And have you, dear," murmured Mrs Cathcart dulcetly to her protégée, "a faithful boy? A swain? A Corydon? An inamorato? A Romeo?"

"Pardon?" said Muriel Figgis.

"Surely, child, some boy has . . . hm?"

"There's Bobby."

"Bobby?"

"Bobby Tomkins."

"Oho. Aha! Bobby. Bobbety. Bob-Bob. Bobbles. Baubles. Balls. Bally-Wallies. And does he . . .? And do you . . .?"

" 'E's iggerant," said Muriel disconsolately. " 'E don't know what it's properly for."

"What, dear, precisely, does he not know what it is for?"

" 'Is sticky-out."

"*Not know what it is for?*"

"Jus' rubbin'. That's as far as 'e got."

"Rubbing! Fancy! But rubbing, you know, is not to be despised. You and I, dear, have had some good rubs, have we not? I picture Bobby having his rub – yes I do! Rub-rub-rub – in bed, perhaps – let us hope he is careful! And do you, dear . . . hm . . . rub him, sometimes, for a treat, also?"

"I 'as done."

"And what, dear, happens – after you have rubbed?"

"Puts me in mind o' toothpaste."

"Young Bobby, I think," said Mrs Cathcart, with that quick and selfless generosity on which the judge at her servants' trial had complimented her, "young Bob-Bob, Bubs, Big Bad Bubbles . . . He needs help, I think? Instruction. Precept. You and I together, dear, must teach him!"

"Oo er," said Muriel.

"Could you not, dearest child, bring him with you, when you visit me next week?"

"Might do," said Muriel significantly.

A nightie, silkette cami-knickers, and a pair of real silk stockings induced Muriel, at last, to promise that she would bring Bobby (if she could! Lads are so wayward!) to Mrs Cathcart's firelit drawing-room.

* * *

Sunday came round again.

Millicent went to early Communion. The neat coppery head was bowed in reverent self-abasement before the altar. She accepted from her father the sacraments of bread and wine, having joined in the General Confession with eyes devoutly closed.

At Matins, she sang as usual in the choir, to Mrs Cathcart's thunderous playing of the organ, like a joyful little bird. Oh, but her voice soared in glad worship up to the ancient vaulting!

"My skylark," murmured Mrs Cathcart, rapt. For, in spite of Muriel, Millicent was, to her, still the pick of the bunch.

Came time for Evensong, and the Vicar off with his incongruous stride, below clouds scurrying in the blusterous wind across a darkening firmament.

But these 'Sunday evening sessions', which had given so much innocent and natural joy, were not what they were. Captain Cathcart had deserted his Millicent; Major Martin; Tom Melhuish from The Black Swan; Jewkes from The Towers, who had gone away to a new position; Doctor Corbishley, who could no longer afford her . . . the only regular customer poor Millicent had was Mr Prynne.

Even he jibbed at the new price – until Millicent promised him, "a lovely new trick to make him giggle."

Afterwards Millicent told Mr Prynne that, before he died, Doctor Bland had given her his collection of snuff boxes. Wasn't it sweet of him? Now she wanted Mr Prynne ever so sweetly to help her sell them. But Mr Prynne made such a fuss! And after she had made him giggle! But of course she persuaded him in the end.

* * *

The brewery put in a new manager at The Black Swan. Even if Melhuish got off, they said, they could not have a rapist as licencee of one of their houses.

The new manager was called Mr Huskisson. He had a wife and one boy, a fair-haired lad of about thirteen.

The village regarded the Huskissons with hostility and suspicion. They were greeted with whispers, averted heads, and scandalous rumours. But the Huskissons did their best, and tried straight away to join in the life of the village, as Tom Melhuish had done.

One of the things they judged it right to do was to send young Jimmy along to the Boys' Club.

* * *

The Boys' Club was the Vicar's opportunity for getting across the glorious message of the gospels directly to the young. "Suffer little children," he often said of his work in the sphere, a phrase which was misunderstood by the simpler among his parishioners. They thought he meant that little children caused him to suffer. They concluded that he was complaining about the unpleasantness, even torment, of contact with their offspring. It made the Vicar, never respected, still more disliked than before.

Tuesday was Boys' Club night. Tuesday, early in the evening, found the Vicar in the War Memorial Hall (an economical structure of corrugated iron) trying to interest a dozen surly, moon-faced village lads in a project to visit lonely old people in the parish.

"So often," he cried to the boys, "we have opportunities for practical Christianity thrust by God under our very noses, and yet we do nothing about it! We're nothing but slackers! What we all want is to turn back our cuffs and get down to it! Isn't that right? Of course it is! I know I do, and I know in your hearts you do, too . . ."

The Vicar's Godly voice, trained into booming sententiousness at the Theological College, faltered and came to a stop. His knees were trembling. He was smitten with a great light, a shaft of the purest radiance . . .

A new recruit had joined the Boys' Club, a fair lad, slender, delicate faced, sitting among the bovine village lads like a Botticelli angel among Breughel peasants, like a slip of a girl among these hulking fellows . . .

The Vicar was borne back down the echoing years on wings of precious memory – back to the one experience of pure happiness in his life – back to the Fifth Form at school – back to Morrison Minor!

He forced himself to carry on, to wear the mask – but had there not been, just for a moment, a glance between Man of God and Lovely Youth, a glance of penetrating sweetness, of understanding, of hope, of expectation?

* * *

"What she want me goin' there *for*?" asked Bobby for the hundredth time.

"Lessons, like," said Muriel obscurely.

"Get enough o' them at school."

"Diffrunt sorta lesson," Muriel informed him, a sly look in her porcine eye.

"What, then?"

"I don't know 'ow it's rightly called. Come *orn*. She still got things I want."

"Yer, well," said Bobby. "You rub me after?"

"Better nor that," said Muriel.

Bobby could imagine nothing better, but this dazzling promise induced him to accede to his fair companion's entreaty. He accompanied Muriel to Mrs Cathcart's, after school on Thursday, when the Kedleston servants were out.

Mrs Cathcart was all delight to see them both, all hospitality with plates of little cakes and fancy biscuits.

They sat in front of the fire in the morning room, the three of them, in the genial light of pink-shaded oil-lamps.

Mrs Cathcart brought the conversation round, ever so delicately, to the subject nearest her heart.

To Muriel (just in passing) she meanwhile promised more silk stockings. To Bobby she offered some things of Captain Cathcart's – a knife with three blades, a leather belt, an army swagger stick.

Bobby saw what Muriel meant. Coming to the old woman's house was lovely!

Then, slowly, he began to understand what she wanted him to do. Her and Muriel, both of them. At first he was simply amazed, then shocked, then deeply abashed, then terrified!

"Neckid?" he gasped. "Nood?"

"It is sweeter, dear boy," Mrs Cathcart assured him.

"But – you'd see me . . ."

"I seen you," Muriel pointed out.

"Yer, but . . ."

"I cannot help you," said Mrs Cathcart, in a voice like treacle, "unless I am here – now can I?"

"Don't want no 'elp," wailed Bobby.

He dug in his toes! He refused! Muriel stamped her foot with vexation, and a frown appeared between Mrs Cathcart's fine eyes.

"You are a naughty, ungrateful boy," she said. "And we know *just* how to deal with *that* sort of behaviour. Come along now, let us have no more of this childish nonsense. If you cannot take your own clothes off, then Mrs Cathcart shall treat you like the baby you are, and take them off for you. Hold his legs, Muriel dear, and I will start with his collar and tie."

How Bobby struggled! But he was powerless in the grasp of the mighty athlete he had thought to defy. Muriel, also, was quite as strong as he was; with her sitting on his legs he was all but helpless.

Off came the belt! Down came the grey school shorts!

"Oh what a little treasure!" cried Mrs Cathcart, enraptured. "So pink at the end! So strong! I declare I could eat it up!"

As though to carry out this whimsical project, Mrs Cathcart lowered her fine head to the 'little treasure', and made as though to gobble it up in truth!

" 'Ere!" croaked Bobby, in terror.

But when she opened her mouth and raised her head, it was still there.

The rest of Bobby's clothes came off, struggle as he might, cry out and blubber and appeal. The rest of his clothes came off, and Mrs Cathcart sat on his chest to keep him quiet.

"Now you, dear," she said to Muriel, who was panting with exertion and excitement.

Be sure that the damsel needed no second bidding!

"There," gurgled Mrs Cathcart. "Now we must bring these two sweet little woolly bears together, and this darling little mouse must go into this darling little mouse-hole waiting for him . . ."

Bobby renewed his struggles – but it was in vain. Mrs Cathcart herself took his sticky-out between finger and thumb, and steered it where, as she said, "all naughty little mice want to go!"

Even then the ungrateful boy did not really enjoy it. Muriel did, although she could see that it might be very much better.

But Mrs Cathcart was in ecstacies. Helping others, as she always said, was her chief joy.

* * *

"I'm goin' to tell on 'er," said Bobby to Muriel, later.

"Aw right," she agreed indifferently. "We don't need 'er no more."

CHAPTER THE THIRTEENTH

In Which A Splinter Thwarts A Noble Resolve

'Telling' on Mrs Cathcart proved to be an immensely gratifying experience.

For the first time in his life, Bobby found himself a hero – the centre of attention – allowed, nay, encouraged, to hold forth at any length, to supply all kinds of details, to elaborate, to repeat, to embroider, to embellish. There was no limit to what people wanted to hear. The more he said, the more they all liked it.

His audience was at first his Dad and Mam only, at supper-time in the cottage behind the Newsagent's. Mr and Mrs Figgis were sent for post-haste, with Muriel. Bobby's story was retold, with additional material. Muriel confirmed it. She said that she herself had been terrified, cowed, probably drugged with something in the little cakes or the fancy biscuits. She said that Mrs Cathcart had threatened her with unspeakable punishments if she breathed a word to anybody. That was why, she explained, she had not mentioned the matter to her parents.

P.C. Flockett was called over. He came reluctantly, having taken off his boots.

The news spread like wildfire through the village. It was

discussed from all angles in the Bar Parlour of The Black Swan – in the kitchens of tradesmen and small-holders – in reeking, overcrowded cottage bedrooms.

The villagers were not imaginative people, owing to poverty of intellect and the absence of any but the most rudimentary education. But the more lurid newspapers had furnished their slow minds, naturally prurient, with a variety of disgusting possibilities; and their own experiences, in farmyard, cowshed and hayloft, had familiarised them with most of the grosser forms of bestiality and perversion.

All that the villagers had read of, heard of, covertly witnessed, or drunkenly attempted was ascribed, in crudely unscientific terminology, to Mrs Cathcart.

By midnight, there was no excess which she did not habitually practise, no humiliation to which she had not subjected her innocent little victims.

In the morning (a fair one, with a gentle breeze, and a bright, clear sky) the other children were jealous of Bobby and Muriel. They, too, wanted some of the glory. Breakfast in dozens of cottages therefore witnessed new and shocking evidence about the depraved mistress of Kedleston. Alf Mallinson remembered a nudge, Mary Quiggs a squeeze, Flo Keep a rumpled head and a murmured invitation. Screams of anger greeted these revelations. More than one mother went into strong hysterics.

Mrs Cathcart's new house-parlourmaid heard a bizarre and highly personal account of her mistress' 'goings-on' from the postman; the cook another, rich in imaginative detail of a scabrous kind, from the milkman. Both servants packed their 'cardboards' and left, without notice, before Mrs Cathcart had so much as rung her bell.

Jangle thy bell in vain, Mrs Cathcart! There shall no

servant come, with tea and letters, ever again, to thy dishonoured couch!

The stoning of Columbine Cottage, which had broken all its windows and driven Dolly Martin away, had given the youths of the village a taste for the delightful music of shattering glass. Only fear of violent punishment had since restrained two or three dozen throwing-arms. The lads longed to break more windows, but they dursn't. Now all restraint was removed. The tall windows of Kedleston were fair game.

By half past ten no ground-floor pane was intact: by eleven o'clock no upstairs one either.

P.C. Flockett laboriously took statements of complaint, to add to those which he already had from Bobby and Muriel. The words almost frizzled the paper. A strongly competitive element entered the recitals. The children of the village realised, with a sure instinct, that so far from being reproved for romancing, they were actually being encouraged to tell the very best stories they could think of.

There were certain adults, too, latent exhibitionists to whom the village had offered no stage on which to indulge their appetite for attention and applause – these pressed forward to old Mrs Flockett's cottage to make their own sworn statements.

The Vicar said, "We must be careful to judge, slow to condemn, quick to understand and forgive. I trust, however, that the abandoned creature will be visited with condign punishment, and incarcerated for the rest of her life *at least*."

Millicent said that she would pray for Mrs Cathcart.

The Vicarage cook sent a pathetic message to Doctor

Corbishley. He was reluctant to visit her, but his sister Edwina reminded him of his duty.

Cook was in her little attic bedroom at the Vicarage. She locked the door when Doctor Corbishley entered, and did to him all the things which rumour said (scarcely credibly) that Mrs Cathcart had done to Bobby Tomkins. Doctor Corbishley cried out in agony that was more physical than spiritual.

Mr Prynne found his hands very full, arranging for Mrs Cathcart's defence, and at the same time disposing quietly of Millicent's valuable collection of antique snuff-boxes.

Tom Melhuish, meanwhile, was further remanded in custody on a charge of rape, and Albert Monger on one of murder. These events, long predicted, were hardly noticed in the village, owing to all the excitement about Mrs Cathcart.

* * *

On Tuesday evening, at the Boys' Club meeting, Bobby Tomkins was still the centre of admiring yet envious attention. Even the Vicar felt obliged to help the lad, if he could, by letting him 'get it off his chest.'

Only one of those present held aloof – uninterested in, or repelled by, the events of the previous Thursday. Young Jimmy Huskisson's lip curled. His delicate eyelids drooped in weary disgust over his clear grey eyes.

The Vicar glanced from the coarse, avid faces of the others, to the interesting pallor of the new recruit. He saw a fine disdain – the suggestion of a shrug.

Either, thought the Vicar, she knows much less about the

sordid side of life than these uncouth boys – or else she knows much more! Not *she*, the Vicar corrected himself hastily. *He*, of course.

Feeling himself stared at (perhaps), Jimmy Huskisson raised his eyes to the Vicar's. His expression remained cool and secret . . . But surely a faint blush mantled those ivory cheeks?

Cheeks, thought the Vicar, in sudden overpowering excitement. Little cheeks, like peeled eggs, smoothest moundlets of an all-egg-smooth body . . . He himself would kneel, with those cheeks turned invitingly towards him. He would place a hand on each, and in an attitude not unlike that of prayer . . .

The Vicar felt his heart thud suffocatingly in his chest, his neck expand until it threatened to burst his dog-collar. He had been, perhaps, a little excited by what he had heard of Bobby's adventures. He had tried to picture the scene – since a priest's first duty is to understand – but he had found himself picturing not so much the scene in general as Bobby in particular . . .

And now Jimmy – in particular! Pale, slender girl-boy, egg-smooth all over, creamy white all over, save for, here and there, haply a touch of pink – hairless as a baby – or perhaps there would be, already, a triangle of soft down, fur of palest gold, silk-fine, exquisite to the touch . . .

Nowhere did the Bible say it was forbidden. The Vicar had searched assiduously, through all Holy Writ, acquiring long ago the reputation of a deep Bible scholar – and nowhere did it say, in so many words, that it was forbidden. Fornication, yes. Adultery, yes. Covering another man's manservant, or his maidservant. Jimmy was no servant, not he, although no doubt he sometimes helped his father at The Black Swan . . .

The lads of the Boys' Club were all looking at Bobby Tomkins. One or two, rendered enthusiastic by his descriptions of Muriel, were busy with their hands in their trouser pockets, their faces abstracted.

Only the Vicar was looking at Jimmy Huskisson, who stood a little apart at the carpentry bench. Jimmy, in turn, was looking at the Vicar. Was there something appraising in his look? Was he asking, with those clear grey eyes, a question? Jimmy glanced round slowly at the others, through half-closed eyes. Only the backs of a dozen bullet heads were turned towards him. As though absent-mindedly, as though his thoughts were far away, as though scarcely aware of what he was doing, he drew up with one pale hand the left leg of his grey flannel shorts, in order to scratch, ever so gently, his slender pearly thigh!

High, high rose the hem of the grey shorts – high over the alabaster skin! With a pink fingernail, unnaturally clean, he scratched as gently as one who would dislodge a fragment of chaff from the downy skin of a ripe peach . . .

Let *me* scratch, screamed the Vicar in his heart.

A boy guffawed, then glanced self-consciously at the Vicar. Other heads turned. Jimmy Huskisson instantly dropped the leg of his shorts back to the dimpled knee where (alas) it belonged. He returned, smiling faintly, to his carpentry.

The mood was broken, the moment ended. But only the Vicar knew that he had been accorded a revelation, or (to put it more simply) been shown a sign.

The little angel (as the Vicar called him in his heart) was a bit of all right. He knew what was what.

The Vicar had no chance of private speech with Jimmy. Nor could he contrive to walk part of the way home with the little lad.

But oh oh oh! Morrison Minor's signal (so long ago, in the Fifth Form classroom) had not been half so frank as Jimmy's.

* * *

Millicent found her father abstracted all evening.

This enabled her the more easily to slip out to meet Mr Prynne in the Mongers' cottage. He gave her £345 in cash for the first batch of snuff-boxes, and another five pounds for, "being Millie's greedy puppy-dog", in the dear girl's own phrase.

* * *

Tom Melhuish came up for trial.

The witnesses for the Prosecution were the Vicarage cook (ravished and blubbering victim of the beastly assault), Mr Jewkes, who from the wheel of the Daimler, and in the glare of its giant electrics, had clearly seen the odious crime in the very midst of its commission, and Doctor Corbishley, who had shortly afterwards examined the victim.

The evidence of Doctor Bland was not, of course, available to the Court, but Prosecuting Counsel felt on firm ground without it.

The Vicarage cook made a deep impression on the Jury. It

was obvious that she was a woman of utter truth and impregnable virtue – no one so repellently ugly could be otherwise.

Mr Jewkes had been brought from far-away Dunstable, where he already occupied a new and respectable position. His evidence, delivered in a lugubrious and convincing bass, corroborated the victim's account of the insane ferocity of the attack.

Doctor Corbishley seemed an ill man. His mind wandered, his voice whined, and sank to an unintelligible whisper. He testified as to the rupture of his patient's hymen, as to torn underclothes and mud, and as to the highly excited, hysterical, abnormal condition of his patient when he examined her.

The Accused was the single witness in his own defence. His story of a shameless invitation from a female in the dark had the worst possible effect on the Jury's view of him. It was not only, they agreed, a patent fabrication, it was also ungallant. Prosecuting Counsel, in his final address to the Jury, made much of this. He invited the Jury to despise the cowardly bully who sought to evade the consequences of his own disgusting crime by besmirching the reputation of a pure and blameless female, member of a Clergyman's household.

Counsel for the Defence was compelled to rely principally on the amount the Accused admitted he had been drinking.

The verdict was a foregone conclusion, the sentence one of exceptional savagery, owing to the bad impression the Accused had made on the Judge as well as the Jury.

* * *

It was, perhaps, the ordeal of giving evidence which pushed Doctor Corbishley at last 'over the edge'.

It was in some ways unfortunate that the moment of collapse should have come while the worthy young Doctor was examining the children of the Infants' School.

Miss Trundle, who had charge of the two dozen apathetic toddlers, was greatly shocked, but at the same time her scholarly bent (which had never deserted her since she had been the swot of her own schooldays) caused her to view with the keenest academic interest the spectacle of a full-grown man (if the skinny little fellow could be so described) attempting self-castration with a wooden ruler entirely unfitted for the purpose. Miss Trundle could have told him where there was a good sharp knife, but judged it best not to 'put her oar in'.

The schoolmarm's first inkling that something untoward was happening was when Doctor Corbishley, in front of all the infants, and in the presence of Miss Trundle herself, undid the buttons of his braces and dropped his trousers to his ankles. This was not usual among visitors to the Infants' School.

He then seized from Miss Trundle's own desk the wooden ruler with which she sometimes drew straight lines, and sometimes 'warmed the botties' of her mischievous charges.

What, thought Miss Trundle, can he want with my ruler?

The infants had watched with their usual apathy the descent of the Doctor's trousers. When he grabbed the ruler, they shrank back, assuming that he intended to punish them with the arbitrary ferocity with which (although they would not have put it in these terms) it seemed to them that their preceptress sometimes belaboured them.

No such thing! The infants were his audience, not his victims.

When the Doctor produced his appendages, there was a flicker of slow interest among some of the children. They had seen such things before, though not in their classroom.

There was more than a flicker of interest from Miss Trundle (though she resolutely hid it), as she had never seen such a thing before, except in statutory, and then with a demure blush.

Miss Trundle's first interpretation was that Doctor Corbishley intended ritual self-circumcision. She had read of such practises in the hardly-credible reports (couched in tactful language) of African travellers. But she observed, as she could scarcely fail to do, that the Doctor was already circumcised, which caused her to change her view. She had always deplored intellectual rigidity in the face of new evidence, and did so still.

Speculation was tinged with amazement when Doctor Corbishley began to saw at himself with the ruler. Miss Trundle was reminded of a cellist (with, to be sure, a short bow and a small 'instrument') furiously playing the *cadenza* of a concerto – left hand clutching the 'instrument', right hand sawing back and forth, and on his face just such an expression of agonised concentration as Miss Trundle had observed in the concert hall.

At last she understood. He was simply trying to cut it off. He was not going about it sensibly. To Miss Trundle's mind he would have done better with a series of sharp blows, or, of course, with a real saw or a carving knife.

She did venture a warning. "I should warn you, Doctor Corbishley," she said gravely, "that there are splinters in that ruler."

She was (in truth) a little ashamed of those splinters, which were her doing. She had used the ruler to guide the blade of a knife, with which she was cutting a piece of cardboard. The knife had slipped more than once into the edge of the ruler. Should Doctor Corbishley be using that edge, and not the other . . .

A howl of pain from the Doctor conveyed to her that the Doctor was, most unfortunately, using the splintery edge. He was impaled!

The children showed more interest. Some of the little girls giggled. Miss Trundle herself was obliged to smile.

"I'm stuck," whimpered Doctor Corbishley, in a voice like no voice Miss Trundle had ever heard a grown man use.

"I did warn you, Doctor," she said, "about the splinters."

In piercing the epidermis of Doctor Corbishley's organ, the splinter had not become detached from its parent ruler. The whole ruler – twelve inches of orange-coloured wood, marked in halves, quarters and eighths – was as it were indissolubly wedded to the somewhat shorter length, cylindrical, of the male part.

"Help!" moaned Doctor Corbishley.

The infants were not hard hearted, though porcine in appearance and bovine in personality. Several rallied to this cry from the heart. Chubby hands grabbed the ruler, others the appendage. Wood and flesh were pulled eagerly this way and that, to detach one from the other.

Doctor Corbishley screamed. The ruler stuck fast. The splinter, long and sharp, still clung in the loose skin.

Miss Trundle was unaffectedly delighted to see her little charges obeying, as they so seldom did, the rule of 'doing unto others', her own often-repeated injunction to 'lend a helping hand'. Little Mavis Foss was literally swinging on the Doctor's organ, clutching it with both baby hands and lifting her feet right off the floor! She was doing all she could to help, no doubt of that. Wilf Vinegar, often a problem boy, was meanwhile yanking the ruler this way and that, with all his strength, to free it.

The fuss the Doctor was making, in Miss Trundle's view, was neither logical nor manly. His intention had unmistakably been to amputate the entire appendage – strike it all off 'at the roots'. A simple splinter, though it might temporarily thwart the effort of amputation, should not in logic have occasioned this clamorous distress. It was not setting a good example to the infants. Miss Trundle always told them "not to make a silly fuss" when they caught their fingers in the door, or wet their knickers (commonest of accidents). She had quoted to them a thousand times the beautiful story of the Spartan boy whose vitals were eaten by a fox. A fine shindy, Miss Trundle austerely thought, Doctor Corbishley would have made, if a fox had begun on *his* vitals.

Miss Trundle believed (for she was in many ways a modern educationalist) that children should do as much as possible on their own – that grown-ups should butt in only when necessary. But at last it became evident to her that the little ones were *not* going to get the splinter out of Doctor Corbishley, and that the moment had come for herself to intervene.

She strode forward, and brushed aside the clutching hands of her pupils. In her left hand she grasped the ruler (her own ruler, after all!) and in her right the piece of pinkish tubing with which Doctor Corbishley was embellished.

Now! A sharp, decisive tug. And a scream of unprecedented shrillness from Doctor Corbishley.

Miss Trundle peered. Surely she had pulled hard enough? Then she had to laugh outright. She had, quite inadvertently, pulled the wrong way! She had driven the splinter deeper into Doctor Corbishley.

"I am afraid," she told him merrily, "I got hold of the wrong end of the stick."

(Telling the story later, as she so often did, this was the moment to which she built. For never before, as she said herself, had she used an ordinary phrase with such extraordinary aptness and felicity – never before come so near that perfection of epigram which marks the great wits of all ages.)

The effect on Doctor Corbishley was unfortunate. He simply rushed out of the school! He could not, of course, run fast, because his trousers were round his ankles, but he made the best speed he could. One hand grasped the ruler, the other its prisoner. He howled continuously.

Miss Trundle was delighted to see the children fall back, politely, to allow the Doctor a clear passage to the door. They. all came very well, Miss Trundle thought, out of the whole episode – and so she told the parents.

* * *

Doctor Corbishley (as it chanced) shuffled straight into the arms of P.C. Flockett, who was on his way to Kedleston to arrest Mrs Cathcart for gross indecency. He arrested Doctor Corbishley for gross indecency first, then proceeded to Kedleston for bigger game.

CHAPTER THE FOURTEENTH

In Which We Take Leave Of Our Friends

Doctor Corbishley was found 'unfit to plead'. He was committed to an institution for the criminally insane 'during His Majesty's pleasure'.

Mrs Cathcart's trial attracted somewhat more publicity. Mr Prynne endeavoured to persuade both the Vicar and his daughter to give evidence as to character. Both declined.

"Character?" cried the Vicar. "Alas. Would you have me testify to the nobility of Jezebel's motives, the purity of Salome's?"

"She shall have my prayers," said Millicent softly. "But I can't get up and tell fibs!"

Nothing Mr Prynne said would shake the child in this high-minded resolve – not even another £480 in cash for the rest of the snuff-boxes, and five pounds on top of that, "for being Millie's naughty doggie, and going down Millie's rabbit-hole."

Mrs Cathcart was sentenced to twelve years. She was given a bad time by the other women prisoners, since many of the criminal classes are good family people.

The Vicar's own arrest, for an attempted offence against the young son of one of his parishioners, caused quite a shock to the neighbourhood. Jimmy Huskisson alone seemed unmoved by the outrage. He smiled secretly, and gave his statement to the police in a clear, mocking treble.

Albert Monger's trial took its predicted course. His Counsel pleaded diminished responsibility, but without success. Albert was hanged at Ludscomb Gaol, protesting to the last, to those who could understand his uncouth mouthings, that the Vicarage young lady had told him to do it.

For a short time the village became quite famous. Lots of newspaper gentlemen came in two-seater cars. Some put up at The Black Swan, until its squalor and discomfort drove them away. Millicent was interviewed and photographed many times. The newspaper gentlemen were charmed by her innocence and piety. Their articles spoke of the pure flame which touches pitch and is not defiled. She became quite a celebrity. As a result, she received eleven offers of marriage through the post, and one offer to star in a cinema film. She replied to six of the proposals of marriage, and was eventually able to make them, with Mr Prynne's help, the basis of 'breach-of-promise' actions, all of which were settled out of court for large sums.

The cinema film she accepted, Mr Prynne having examined and amended the contract. The film was made, but never shown to the public, as Millicent did not, for all her elfin charm, seem to photograph well. She gave the impression of lumpiness, and had no talent for acting. But she became great friends with the producer of the film, who was quite an elderly gentleman.

On her sixteenth birthday she married the producer of the cinema film. At seventeen, widowed, she bought The Towers from Doctor Bland's executors. She entertained lavishly but discreetly, involving herself (wicked puss) in a series of hardly credible adventures.

Jimmy Huskisson became one of Millicent's frequent visitors at The Towers, a circumstance which had a notable effect on his remarkable subsequent career.

Muriel Figgis had a baby. She said that the father was her father, not, as had generally been supposed during the pregnancy, Bobby Tomkins. This accusation turned out to be true, which occasioned the ostracism of the Figgis family, their bankruptcy, and their removal in misery to distant parts.

Bobby Tomkins never did acquire a taste for what Mrs Cathcart had taught him. He was quite put off it. He preferred 'rubbing' until the end of his life, remaining, in consequence, prosperous and cheerful.

Columbine Cottage remained unsold. It stood empty, becoming more and more derelict, until burnt down as a 'lark' by the lads of the village. Dolly Martin had meanwhile secured a post as chambermaid in a 'Family and Commercial Hotel' in a Midland town. She gave tolerable satisfaction, though was never fully accepted by her fellow servants, until she contracted an unmentionable disease from one of the male guests, and transmitted it to another. She later sold matches with moderate success outside the railway station, a career terminated when she was run over by a lorry.

Queenie Perkup entered her mother's profession, at the age of thirteen, at her grandmother's suggestion. She was joined by Mabel and Phyllis as soon as they were old enough, or, to be lamentably exact, rather sooner than they were old enough.

The association between Queenie and Jimmy Huskisson

was not, perhaps, morally beneficial to either. But that, as Mr Kipling used to say, is another story.

Vic Mallinson killed, butchered, minced and sold his old pony, Bluebell. A number of deaths in the village were shortly thereafter attributable to sausages from Mallinson's, but by bribing Doctor Bland's successor, Vic evaded prosecution. His new pony stopped in a different place when he came back drunk from Bogham on Sunday nights. So he never found Mrs Cathcart's other suitcase, or the trunk, arms and feet of Captain Cathcart.

Miss Trundle of the Infant's School at last recovered her ruler from the police, and uses it still, both for drawing lines and for chastisement.

Farewell